"Our Discussion Is At An End, Patricia," Marc Said. "For God's Sake, Go To Bed!"

His rejection a blow that shattered her budding self-confidence, she didn't struggle when he eased her into a sitting position on his lap.

"I'm sorry I went to that stupid dinner party tonight, Marc. I knew you'd be angry, but I—I never meant this to happen."

Her gentle apology did nothing to ease the guilt tearing him apart inside. "If it means anything," he muttered tiredly, "my own behavior was way out of line."

Suddenly hopeful, Patricia tried to reassure him. She hesitantly lifted her hand and placed it gently against the rigid curve of his jaw.

Marc recoiled violently, and hope died in her breast as her hand fell to her side. "Why do you always shut me out?" she whispered. "Why do you lock yourself away in a place where I can't follow?"

When he spoke, his voice was a harsh rasp. "Because I don't want to be reached, my dear."

Dear Reader,

April is here and spring is in the air! But if you aren't one of those lucky people who gets to spend April in Paris, you can still take that trip to romance—with Silhouette Desire!

You can fly off to San Francisco—one of *my* favorite cities!—and meet Frank Chambers, April's *Man of the Month,* in *Dream Mender* by Sherryl Woods. Or you can get into a car and trek across America with Brooke Ferguson and Pete Cooper in *Isn't It Romantic?* by Kathleen Korbel. (No, I'm not going to tell you what Pete and Brooke are doing. You have to read the book!) And if you're feeling particularly adventurous, you can battle fish, mud and flood with Dom Seeger and Alicia Bernard in Karen Leabo's delightful *Unearthly Delights.*

Of course, we all know that you don't *have* to travel to find love. Sometimes happiness is in your own backyard. In Jackie Merritt's *Boss Lady,* very desperate and very pregnant TJ Reese meets hometown hunk Marc Torelli. Tricia Everett finds that the man of her dreams is . . . her husband, in Noelle Berry McCue's *Moonlight Promise.* And Caroline Nobel returns to the man who's always lit her fire in *Hometown Man* by Jo Ann Algermissen.

So, it might not be April in Paris for you—*this* year. But don't worry, it's still love—at home or away— with Silhouette Desire.

Until next month,

Lucia Macro
Senior Editor

NOELLE BERRY McCUE

MOONLIGHT PROMISE

SILHOUETTE *Desire*®

Published by Silhouette Books New York

America's Publisher of Contemporary Romance

SILHOUETTE BOOKS
300 East 42nd St., New York, N.Y. 10017

MOONLIGHT PROMISE

ISBN: 0-373-05707-5

First Silhouette Books printing April 1992

Printed in the U.S.A.

NOELLE BERRY McCUE,

who helped launch the Silhouette Desire line under the pseudonym Nicole Monet, lives in California. "I've always loved to read," the author says, "and writing has filled a void in me I was never consciously aware of having. It has added depth to my life and a greater awareness and appreciation of the people around me. With every book I write, I hope I am in some small way paying for the pleasure reading has given me over the years. If I can help just one person find enjoyment and release from everyday troubles, then I've accomplished my purpose in my chosen field."

The author concludes by saying, "That's why I write romances, because they leave the reader with a positive attitude toward love, life and relationships. When all is said and done, isn't it love for others that gives us the greatest happiness in life?"

One

Marcus Everett covered the distance from the departure lounge of San Francisco's international airport to the baggage claim area with impatient strides, his chiseled, boldly defined features etched in lines of weariness. He wasn't a handsome man. His nose was a bit too prominent, his mouth too wide, and his chin, even with the saving grace of a deep dimple cleft in its center, was a mite too square for classical beauty. Thanks to a long-ago Cherokee ancestor, his hair was thick and straight and as black as sin; his piercingly intense eyes deep-set and the color of rich, dark chocolate.

That those almond-shaped eyes were framed by a long, double thick fringe of sooty lashes he found immaterial, but for the women who came in contact with them they were mesmerizing. So, too, was the unconscious sensuality apparent in his slow, loose-hipped walk, and the pride inherent in his posture. Add to those attributes dark, mahogany tanned skin and a body in peak physical condition, and the end result was a man with enough sex appeal to draw the gaze of most females. As was the case now, for several women turned to follow his progress through the crowd. Since he also topped six foot six and had shoulders like a linebacker, this was an easy task to accomplish.

The most likely word to describe Marcus Everett would be "impressive." Or "formidable," if you happened to be in his employ. He was a hard taskmaster who didn't suffer fools at all, but was unfailingly fair in his dealings with his staff. He carried his own work load with admirable stamina, and never asked anyone for more than they could reasonably give to their job. As founder and head of the Everett Property Management and Development Corporation, a multinational property management and investment firm, he was always attuned to the welfare of his people. This responsibility he handled with ease, and a cool efficiency under stress that was almost legendary.

Marc looked neither right nor left as he navigated the crowded thoroughfare, his quick, decisive mind fixed firmly upon his goal. Forging ahead regardless of any obstacles in his path was a familiar scenario for him, and one in which he excelled. The son of a

Pennsylvania coal miner, he had risen from the squalor of his childhood to the top of the corporate ladder with ruthless determination, and a self-confident obstinacy that had gained him grudging respect among the more elite, blue blooded members of the international business community.

That it had also gained him a fair number of enemies along the way he viewed as a regrettable, if unavoidable, necessity. Rigidly individualistic and for the most part a loner, he didn't really care what anyone thought of him. A self-made man, with the emphasis on "made," he had long ago learned that gouging his mark on the world was what mattered, as were the resultant wealth and power—which were as necessary to him as breathing—and the certainty that never again would he be one of life's victims.

"Mr. Everett!"

His exhaustion-dazed mind snapped to attention at the sound of the familiar, distinctive voice, and his head snapped up as he scanned the cavernous lower level in search of his quarry. To his left, there was a large group of what appeared to be Japanese businessmen, and a multiracial conglomerate of travelers huddled around a constantly rotating, circular metal depository in front of him, which was monotonously engorged with luggage dropped from a droning overhead conveyor belt.

As he squinted to clear his vision, the motley buzz of various languages being spoken assaulted both his ears and his head. His stomach churned in accompanying rebellion, his system disoriented by too many time zones crossed in too little time. These past few days had seen him traveling from the warmth of the Bahamian coast to the oppressive heat of New York City in mid-summer, where his firm's central offices were located. Then it was back to the more moderate clime of northern California.

Now he was most anxious to reach the comfortable, elegant sanity of his home, and to be relaxed by the capable ministrations of his wife Patricia. It was her practice to greet him at the door with a welcoming smile and a soothing word, which was why he always wired ahead with news of his intended arrival. Although it galled him to admit it, he had come to rely on his wife's quiet, sensible presence to balance his grueling work schedule. But since it was the only dependency he allowed himself, he shrugged the knowledge aside.

Marc suddenly pictured Patricia's cool, Nordic beauty in his mind and felt his body tighten responsively. A wry smile twisted the corners of his mouth, and he found himself marveling at the recuperative powers of the human mind and body. One moment his thoughts were vague and disjointed with exhaustion, and the next his imagination was gearing him for action. Of course after nearly a month of endless meetings and impersonal hotel rooms, it wasn't surprising that relaxing wasn't all he had on his mind.

"Here, sir," the voice cried out once again. "Over here by the gate."

But Marc had already located the balding head and toothy grin of his chauffeur/handyman among the shifting sea of strangers, and he made his way toward the exit gate with relieved alacrity. Eyeing the assorted baggage at the rotund man's feet, he said, "One step ahead of me as usual, Cully."

A touch of his cockney heritage still evident in his speech the other man responded, "Can't say as how I haven't had a bit of practice, sir."

Handing the nearby airport official his baggage claim receipts, Marc waited while the uniformed man compared the numbers to those affixed on his luggage. Pushing aside the loose folds of his gray, lightweight sports coat, he shoved his hands into the pockets of trim black slacks and restlessly jingled the loose change he found there. With barely restrained impatience, he asked, "How are things at home, Cully? Have you and Martha become grandparents yet?"

Edward Culcahy's heavily jowled chin quivered as he shook his head, his twinkling brown eyes belying the disgusted expression on his face. "Not a bit of it, sir. As you remember, our Mary Lynn was always a stubborn little madam, and it looks as though her offspring ain't going to be much better. Two weeks overdue she is, and as big as a pickle barrel. It's a good thing you built our girl and her Ben that house on the estate last year, or we'd really be in a fix."

"Why is that?" Marc inquired with an absentminded lift of one mobile brow.

Reacting to an impersonal nod from the airport official, he didn't pause to wait for a reply to his question. Grasping the leather handles of the two bags nearest him, he rapidly passed through the exit gate leading back onto the main concourse. Cully bent to gather together the other bags, and automatically followed his employer through the baggage claim area.

With the ease of familiarity Marc merged with others seeking to depart the airport, the hollow echo of their footsteps suiting the cavernous impersonality of their surroundings. Without hesitation he shifted to the right and stepped onto an automated conveyor, which conveniently lessened the walking distance from the airport's main terminal building to the garage area.

Placing the heavy leather cases at his feet, he straightened and surreptitiously stretched his aching back muscles. Then he glanced over his shoulder at a panting Cully, and once again arched an inquiring brow in his direction. Responding to the unspoken question, Cully's burly chest expanded on an indrawn breath as he eyed his employer with morose intensity. "If my Martha couldn't slip on over to Mary Lynn's whenever the notion took her there'd be hell to pay, that I don't doubt. You'd be minus a housekeeper and I'd be listing myself as a bachelor on my income tax forms, danged if I wouldn't!"

Marc kept a quirk from indenting the corner of his mouth by tightly compressing his lips. When he felt he could safely do so, he remarked, "That bad, huh?"

Nodding with a force that set his jowls to quivering again, Cully muttered glumly, "You'd think a woman who'd had three kids of her own would take becoming a grandmother in stride, but not Martha Jane Culcahy. She's been as sour as an unripe persimmon this past month, that she has. If Mary Lynn so much as sneezes, her mother's all over her like pollen on a bee's legs. She's had hysterics twice already this week, and the last time I tried to talk some sense into her she made me sleep on the couch. I tell you, Marcus, a man can only take so much female foolishness in his stride!"

This last was said with such a despondent note, Marc was hard-pressed to maintain his equanimity. When Cully called him by his first name in public, he knew the old man's emotions had gotten the best of him. Generally he insisted upon maintaining a strict employer/employee relationship, his pride in his professional status of utmost importance in his life. But once in a while he forgot to stand on his dignity, and a trace of the neighbor who had been his father's best friend bled through. Especially, Marc realized with an inward surge of amusement, when Cully's wife was the subject under discussion.

His forty-odd years of wedded bliss to a woman as strong-minded as she was soft-hearted had never run smooth, and the Culcahys fought and loved with almost equal ferocity. Where Cully was reserved, Martha was outgoing, where he was quiet, she was a veritable chatterbox, and whenever his masculine ego demanded he push, Martha shoved him back into place without effort. That volatile yet devoted relationship had been one of the few constants in Marc's life, and one he would never willingly jeopardize by taking sides.

They had reached the end of the moving walkway, and as he bent to grip the handles of his suitcases he was glad he had his back to the older man. If Cully caught sight of the grin he was no longer able to suppress, Marc knew he could look forward to a long spell of formality from his long-time friend and mentor. Being "yes sir'd" and "no sir'd" to death wasn't a prospect he looked forward to, especially from the man who had taught him the meaning of dignity in the face of adversity. With a tramp for a mother and a drunk for a father, he thought with sudden bitterness, it was a lesson he'd needed to learn in order to escape from the degradation and squalor of his childhood.

Once they reached the elevators and climbed to the fourth level, it took only moments to reach the gleaming silver BMW parked in one of the clearly marked spaces nearby. Throwing his luggage into the trunk with little regard for its designer quality, he yawned and pressed both hands against the ache in the back of his neck. "I feel as though I could sleep for a week," he muttered tiredly. "God, but the idea of lying in my own bed for a change sounds good!"

Cully cast him a sideways glance as he unlocked the passenger door. "Wouldn't do Mrs. Everett no harm to have you around more, either. That big house gets mighty lonely with just her to rattle around in it, I'll be bound.''

Marc scrutinized his companion's studied bland features with suspicion, arrested by the personal nature of the remark. In chillingly soft tones he asked, ''Are you trying to tell me something, Cully?''

With a derisive snort the other man circled the car, using the excuse of needing to unlock his own door to avoid his employer's eyes. But once seated within the contoured luxury of the driver's seat, worry for the man at his side overcame his usual discretion. ''Miss Patricia's been a tad restless lately, and she don't smile near as much as she used to, Marcus.''

As he busied himself with his own seat belt, Marc felt the familiar tension coiling through his body at this reference to his wife's increasingly obvious discontent. ''I can't imagine why, unless that diamond bracelet I brought back from my last trip wasn't enough to please her refined taste in jewelry. I'll have to have a matching necklace made to go with it next time around.''

Only silence greeted his sarcastic remark, which was no more than he'd expected. Because of the closeness of their past association Cully might throw him a hint or two if he thought it necessary, but he would never openly interfere in his employer's relationship with his wife. As the car was put into gear, Marc slumped back against the supporting curvature of the butter-soft leather bucket seat and lowered his lashes. Immediately his wife's aloof blue eyes and patrician features rose up to tantalize his mind, and he felt his hands clench in automatic response.

When he'd asked Patricia Ann Sinclair to marry him he had been completely honest and up-front about his expectations. He respected and admired her, but if she desired a romantic approach to their relationship she was going to be disappointed in him. "I am a pragmatic man, Patricia. I consider outpourings of true love to be nonsensical drivel created by weak-willed people to justify indulging their basic biological urges," he'd stated firmly, "and nor do I believe in basing a relationship solely on sexual compatibility."

He wanted a woman of impeccable background, he had continued, who was well educated, self-assured, and conversant with the social graces, who would manage his home and entertain his guests with the elegance befitting a lady. Not a woman like his mother had been, he'd thought at the time, an earthy beauty with the morals of an alley cat and the soul of a harlot. He envisioned a marriage based on reality and mutual respect, not one that forced a good man to hide from his pain and disillusion at the bottom of a bottle of cheap whiskey.

Tricia had greeted his proposal with the quiet dignity so inherent in her nature, and the assurance that she understood his viewpoint. "As the daughter of a retired U.S. senator and the sister of a lawyer, I'm used to dealing with men who know their own minds," she had admitted with a demure smile. "Although I don't entirely agree with your philosophy regarding marriage, I, too, wish to be able to respect and admire the man I marry."

"With what don't you agree?"

She lowered her eyes to the pristine white linen cloth covering the table at which they sat, and traced the stem of her wineglass with absentminded precision. She seemed oblivious to the muted conversations being indulged in by the other diners nearby, her concentration focused solely on the movements of her slim, manicured finger. "I believe a man and woman should love each other before making a lifetime commitment, Marc."

Bristling with defensiveness, he barely managed to keep his voice from reflecting his disappointment in her. Instead he murmured, "Just what is your definition of 'love,' Patricia?"

"For me the word comprises affection, devotion, and tenderness toward someone or something other than ourselves," she replied without hesitation. "That's the kind of relationship my parents enjoy, and it's what I want for myself."

"And don't you think I feel that way toward you?"

She looked up at him then, and he was lost within the gentle depths of her vivid blue eyes. "Do you, Marcus?"

With a nod he leaned forward, and stilled the restless movement of her hand with his own. "Come home with me," he coaxed huskily, "and let me show you how I feel."

Her eyes widened briefly before her long, sweeping lashes lowered to hide her expression. Then she slowly rose to her feet, her tall, slender body appearing oddly defenseless as she faced him across the table. "I'll wait for you in the foyer."

That night he had been disconcerted to discover the full extent of her innocence, but shock had quickly given way to bemused delight. He had soothed her fears and patiently taught her to respond to his demands, and had been rewarded by soft sighs and weakly clinging arms. Her uncertainty and the unavoidable pain he caused her had precluded a more passionate response, but that was no more than he'd expected from a woman with her shy, restrained nature.

Afterward he gathered her languid body close to his side, and studied the face resting against his shoulder. Her lashes formed twin fans against her flushed cheeks, her exquisitely molded features as composed as he'd come to expect. "You should have told me you'd never been with a man before," he admonished her gently.

"Would it have made any difference?"

Her lashes lifted to reveal the crystal purity of her gaze, and there was an expression in her eyes that disconcerted him. It was a look of resignation . . . almost of sadness, and he hardened himself against the quick surge of guilt that rose up inside of him at her vulnerability. Using her question as a distraction, his reply was blunt and to the point. "No, it wouldn't. In fact, quite the opposite, I would say. Virginity is a rare commodity these days, and should be valued accordingly."

The laugh he uttered held more cynicism than amusement, and she flinched at the sound. "Is that what I am to you, a commodity?" she asked quietly.

He ran his hand over her smooth shoulder, his palm pausing to rest against the pulse beat at her throat. "You are a delight," he corrected hoarsely, "while I'm a hard-edged bastard who can be ruthless when necessary. If I wasn't, you wouldn't be in my bed right now. You're like a fragile white rose who has been protected from the harsher elements of life, while I am the storm intent on ripping you from the safety you've always known. If I had an ounce of compassion in me, I'd have left you alone."

"I wasn't unwilling," she reminded him.

"You gave yourself to me, but make no mistake about it, Patricia. If you hadn't I'd have changed your mind, one way or another."

She shivered at the implacable intent in his words. "And do you always get what you want?" she questioned in barely audible tones.

With ruthless honesty, he bit out, "Always!"

His eyes narrowed as the color drained from her cheeks, the sight causing his fingers to tighten against her reflexively. The extent of his emotional reaction to her surprised him, but he carefully loosened his grip on her throat. She was too delicate for rough handling, and he'd never deliberately damage that creamy flesh with marks of possessiveness.

Yet he did feel possessive toward her, he realized, and had from the moment he'd first laid eyes on her. He'd walked into the office of one of his apartment managers, and come face to face with a vision so exquisite he'd felt poleaxed. Instantly his primitive instincts had screamed "She's mine," although he was careful to make certain that Patricia had no idea of the emotional impact she'd had on him.

And nor would she, he vowed silently, even as he pulled her closer into his embrace. He was a healthy male who had reacted normally to her blond loveliness, not some lovesick fool without the self-control and good sense to appreciate her more sterling qualities. But unfortunately, those very qualities of gentleness and caring made her a threat to him, and the knowledge of his own vulnerability made him angry.

Her sweetly giving nature was a subtle lure, calling forth the idealistic boy he'd once been and would never be again. She was the antithesis of his selfish, calculating mother, which was why he was drawn to her so strongly. But even so, he wouldn't allow himself to become emotionally dependent on anyone, especially a woman. That road led only to destruction, as his father had finally proven in a way his son could never forgive or forget.

"Don't look like that, Marc."

Taking a deep breath and pausing to regain his control, he smiled with wry detachment. "Like what, a bad-tempered brute?"

She shook her head, while her fingers began to trace the rigid angle of his jaw. "Like a man who's lost his soul."

Her analogy shook him to the core, but he covered his reaction with forced amusement. "And are you going to help me find it, my golden-haired Madonna?"

Her hand stilled against the side of his face. There wasn't a trace of levity in her expressive features as she gazed up at him and whispered, "I think I must."

Turning his head to press a kiss against her palm successfully shielded his own expression from her far too discerning gaze. "Then you'll marry me?"

With a barely noticeable pause she gave him the response he coveted. "Yes," she murmured, her voice a soft but firm promise in the moonlight-speared darkness of the room. "Yes, I'll marry you, Marc."

Their engagement had been a whirlwind of activity, which had precluded further confidences of that sort, a circumstance he had greeted with profound relief. He was a self-contained man, and soul searching didn't sit well on his shoulders. So he had concentrated on clearing his calendar, giving his business responsibilities most of his time and concentration. Patricia had shown her understanding by assuming the mantle of authority regarding their wedding arrangements, and he had approached his wedding day with the confidence and complacency of a man who was well pleased with his choice of a bride.

"But is she as pleased with her choice of a husband?" an inner voice now taunted derisively. He shied away from the question, shifting his weight restlessly as the car accelerated onto the freeway.

Although he didn't want to admit it, Cully had hit the nail on the head when he'd remarked on Patricia's strange restlessness lately. There was something going on in that beautiful head of hers, and being unable to figure out what was bothering her was making him edgy. She'd always been reserved and somewhat reticent with him, but the past few months had seen a marked deterioration in their relationship.

They seldom made love anymore. The fault was his, but was it any wonder? he thought cynically, feeling the frustrated tightening of his body with familiar resentment. Realizing a woman endured rather than enjoyed a man's touch did rather sting his male pride, and attempts to justify her attitude wasn't much solace when he was aching and hungry. When he did give in and reach for her it was usually more of a hurried attempt to appease his appetite than it was lovemaking, and she no longer even tried to hide her relief when it was over.

What in hell did she expect from him? he asked himself with impatience. He was not a man who worked from nine to five and returned home to dance attendance on his wife, a fact she'd been well aware of before she married him. All right, so maybe his business trips had increased in length and frequency over the past year or so. The size of his corporate holdings had grown in proportion to his time away from home, and it wasn't as though he alleviated his sexual cravings with other women when he was gone.

Although he'd been tempted, he admitted with wry honesty. Marc's time away had been spent negotiating a merger with a Bahamian hotel chain, and the newest contract lawyer hired by his firm had left him in no doubt as to her availability or the lack of emotional strings attached to her offer of companionship. Alita Murray was a career woman first and foremost, but she had a healthy sexual appetite she took no trouble to hide. Her sensual nature was explicitly conveyed by the sinuous sway of her hips when she crossed a room, and in the avid conjecture in her gaze when she looked at a man she found attractive.

That he found her sexually provocative didn't surprise him, considering the self-control he exercised with his wife. Keeping in mind her sheltered upbringing and her rather cold nature, he was careful to repress his baser instincts around Patricia. She deserved respect and consideration, not the heated, hungry sex he'd indulged in with other women before his marriage. If he sometimes longed for more unrestrained passion and spontaneity in their physical relationship, well . . . that was his problem.

Frustration built inside him, carried by a steady flow of self-disgust. Pressing his fingers against the pain viciously slicing into his temples, he forced himself to breathe deeply and evenly. He had no right to decry a relationship that he, himself, had molded into the sterile mockery of what it might have been. Nor should he be comparing Patricia with other women, when she was exactly what he'd wanted in a wife.

He was just suffering from jet lag, he decided in an attempt to justify his thoughts as he slipped deeper into the cushioned comfort of the bucket seat. There was probably a simple reason for Patricia's recent moodiness, and he had a good idea what it might be. When they were first married she'd often suggested that she accompany him on his frequent trips, but he had always put her off. He preferred keeping his home life separate and inviolate from that of his business existence. Eventually she'd stopped asking to go with him.

Could boredom be at the root of the problem? he wondered dispiritedly. He was going to have to return to the Bahamas in a few weeks to sign the final papers on this merger, and it was lovely there this time of year. Patricia could soak up some sun while he completed his business transactions, and their evenings could be spent together. He'd discuss the possibility with her when he got home, he decided with tired resolve.

Marc's eyelids were growing heavier by the minute, his body finally reaching that weightless plane of relaxation, which for him was a forerunner to sleep. As he slipped deeper into somnolence, a slight softening eased the strain from his mouth as he pictured his wife against a backdrop of white sand and foam-flecked surf, her blond hair loose and blowing free in the wind.

Two

Tricia carefully closed the heavy front door behind her and slid the bolt lock into place as quietly as possible. She hadn't been aware of holding her breath until she exhaled on a sigh, and as she turned to cross the cavernous, white and gray tiled entry hall, there was a rather piquant smile curving her lips. When Marc joined her at breakfast in the morning there would be nothing to smile about, but apparently his jet lag had caught up with him as she'd thought it would. She had planned this evening down to the last detail, but she was beginning to realize that rebellion didn't automatically instill the rebel with courage.

The entry hall was lighted by the huge crystal chandelier inset into a thirty-foot ceiling, but the dimmer switch was turned to its lowest setting. The long hallway was eerily shadowed, and she shivered as her shoes echoed her tiptoeing footsteps. Pausing at the bottom of the gray carpeted stairs, she reached out to balance herself on a wide, intricately carved oak railing and removed her sling-back pumps. The three-inch heels were higher than she normally wore and her feet were killing her...as Marc had probably wanted to do when he arrived home tonight to find her gone.

The thought increased her tension, but she staunchly pushed the worry aside. Let him be angry, she decided with careless insouciance, reminding herself that her night out had been geared for just such a reaction. She sighed as she slipped out of the silk-lined black cape jacket she was wearing, and flung the discarded covering over the newel-posted stair railing. At least when he was angry she managed to gain his full attention, and it was time he learned that she was more than a pretty ornament to be dusted off and fondled whenever he felt the urge.

"I'd like to see you in the library for a few minutes, Patricia."

The calm, even tone of her husband's voice startled her even more than a shout would have, and she uttered a muted squeak as she swiveled to look at him. He was standing in the oval archway leading into the library, his imposing figure framed by the darkly polished double doors. As she took in the carefully controlled expression on his swarthy face, she swallowed with difficulty.

Nervously clearing her throat of the sudden constriction blocking her vocal chords, she stammered, "I—I'm rather t—tired, Marc."

"I imagine you are," he interjected softly. "After all, it is nearly midnight."

"Um, yes, well . . ."

"In here, if you please," he said, gesturing at the room behind him with a deceptively negligent hand. "This won't take long, my dear."

The "my dear" was a definite tip-off, and for the first time she noticed the dark blood mottling his rigidly compressed jaw. Marc wasn't angry, he was absolutely, unequivocally, unquestioningly furious. Just how long did it take for a man to strangle a woman? she wondered on the verge of hysteria, slipping past his large, intimidating body on feet that suddenly seemed to grow wings. One minute . . . two? If the way he was looking at her was any indication, she decided breathlessly, it wouldn't take him more than thirty seconds to accomplish the task.

As soon as she entered the library, with a richly detailed Turkish carpet covering its hardwood floor and stately floor-to-ceiling bookshelves lining two of its longest walls, she knew why she hadn't been tipped to his presence by a light shining under the door. Obviously Marc had been sitting in the dark, with only the leaping flames from the fireplace to illuminate his surroundings. It didn't bode well for the state of his temper.

Tricia hated the thought of conducting an argument in this, her favorite room in the house. When they were first married she had spent long, pleasant hours deciding on just the right furniture to grace its sweeping, elegant lines. It had taken her forever to find the delicately structured Regency desk in the corner by the tall, rose damask-draped windows, and almost as much time to choose furniture that wouldn't clash with the room's mellow ambiance. She had decided to place two large wing chairs in front of the fireplace. They were upholstered in the same brilliant blue detailed in the carpet, and were separated by a Regency end table that had belonged to an English great-great-grandmother.

Unfortunately, the library failed to have its usual calming effect upon her nerves. Even the warmth from the fireplace couldn't subdue the chill pervading her body, and she shook revealingly as she headed in its direction. Placing her rhinestone beaded handbag on the dark, ornately carved antique mantel, she held her hands out to the flickering fire and did her best to ignore her husband's brooding presence behind her.

Although the house had been constructed with forced air heating as well as air-conditioning, Marc enjoyed the soothing beauty of an open blaze. So when their home was being designed he had insisted upon reconciling modern-day comfort with the charm of the past, and the architect had installed fireplaces in several rooms, all of which could be lighted or doused with the flick of an electric switch. She had been entranced by the amazingly realistic artificial logs stacked upon raised, wrought-iron grates, and she remembered how he had laughed at her fascination as she had playfully turned the switch on and off.

Only he wasn't laughing now, that was for certain. As she glanced over her shoulder at him his face seemed to be carved in granite, and the tenseness of his body was revealed by snug-fitting black cords and the short-sleeved black sports shirt that clung to the massive contours of his chest. Her glance slid furtively upward until she was once again studying his face, and she almost moaned aloud at what she saw. His lips were tightly compressed, his piercing black eyes smouldering with restrained fury.

But his deep voice was confusingly bland as he asked, "Did you enjoy your evening, darling?"

Dragging a shaken breath into her lungs, she turned and seated herself in one of the plump, comfortable wing chairs. Trying desperately to appear relaxed, she leaned back and crossed one long, nylon-clad leg over the other. As she smoothed the skirt of her figure-hugging cream wool dress, she noticed how badly her hand was shaking.

Praying that he wouldn't notice such an unmistakable indication of vulnerability, she lifted her face to his with a proud toss of her head. "I had a very nice time, thank you. How was your flight?"

Marc ignored the question, his cold gaze inspecting her unrevealing features with intensity. "Martha didn't seem to know where your dinner party was being held."

Tilting her chin to a defiant angle, she clasped her hands tightly together in her lap. "That's because I didn't tell her," she replied with a calm she was far from feeling. "I'm not answerable to Martha for my whereabouts, Marc."

"To Martha, or to anyone?" he questioned silkily. "Aren't you answerable to your husband?"

"My husband rarely discusses his own activities when he's away from home, which is most of the time. I don't see why I should behave any differently."

His voice as smooth and soft as melted butter, he remarked, "A case of tit for tat, my dear?"

Tricia gulped down a sudden surge of panic. "Not at all," she corrected quickly. "Attending a small dinner party was hardly an act of revenge."

"Since you sent Cully to the airport to meet me, I assume you received my telegram stating the date and time of my arrival?"

Both statement and accusation, Tricia felt herself bristling at his words. If she accomplished nothing else from this particular encounter, she decided stalwartly, she would make certain that Marc realized the days of her being at his beck and call were over. Nor was she going to continue catering to his wishes at the expense of her own. She was through being a doormat.

"I knew you were arriving tonight," she finally told him, "but I accepted this engagement weeks ago. I didn't see any reason to cancel at the last minute."

Something heated and dangerous leaped in his eyes, and he leaned forward and braced his hands on the arms of her chair. "Didn't you, my darling wife? Even knowing that I expected you to be here when I arrived?"

Her body went rigid at the sudden closeness between them, but she refused to cringe against the cushion behind her like a sniveling coward. Firming her lips until their lushly full outline thinned repressively, she said, "If you remember, when we married I had the minister remove 'obey' from the service."

Marc perched his hip upon the thickly padded arm of her chair, and balanced himself by draping his forearm over its rounded back. His left hand gently began tucking a few errant strands of hair back into the golden coronet she wore, the elegant simplicity of the style suiting her Nordic loveliness in a way a more modern hairdo would never have achieved. "I thought it amusing at the time," he confided absentmindedly.

There he goes again, she thought, more irritated than usual by his refusal to take her seriously. "That isn't all you found amusing about the ceremony," she snapped. "Don't think I didn't notice the cynical smirk on your face when you vowed to love and honor me, Marcus."

"Ah, you always use my full name when you're angry," he said. "Why are you mad at me, dearest heart?"

Unreasonably disappointed when, instead of denying her remark, he chose to respond with that mocking, sarcastic drawl she loathed, she gritted her teeth to prevent herself from screaming at him like a fishwife. Angrily pushing his hand aside, she lunged to her feet. As she wheeled around to face him, she shouted, "Don't be so damned facetious!"

"You're right. There's nothing in the least humorous about this discussion." His features hardened with resolve, his gaze sharpening on her anger-flushed face. "That being the case, would you like to tell me what you're trying to prove by tonight's foolishness?"

"Foolishness?" she gasped, his question provoking her into further adversity. "You call asserting my rights as an intelligent human being foolish?"

"It's your behavior that's foolish," he muttered disparagingly. "And I've never once questioned your intelligence, Patricia."

Wrapping her arms around herself, she gripped her elbows and began pacing in front of him with visible agitation. She was staring blindly into space, her movements uncharacteristically uncoordinated as she retorted, "No, just my rights as a human being are in question."

With an exasperated sigh, Marc slid sideways into the chair she'd just vacated and slung a single leg over its arm. Swinging his upraised foot while he tapped the other against the floor in a restless rhythm, he laid his head against the protruding wing and studied his wife's militant stance with jaundiced eyes. "For God's sake, what are you talking about, woman? I'm too damn tired right now to attempt reading your mind."

"When have you ever cared what was in my mind?" she demanded, her voice cracking with repressed emotion. "As far as you're concerned, I don't have an original thought in my head. It's you who decides where I go, how I act, who I associate with. Well I'm fed up, do you understand me? I'm sick to the teeth of being the proper, charmingly correct, sweetly boring Mrs. Marcus Everett."

"What's wrong in a wife striving to please her husband?"

"Nothing," she retorted, "as long as the striving is a mutual enterprise."

His jaw tautened grimly. "Meaning?"

"Meaning that it's time you started considering what *I* want for a change."

"Ah," he breathed in enlightenment. "So I was right about the reason for your recent behavior."

Tricia stared at him, her expression puzzled. "I don't know what you mean."

"You've been moody as hell for months now, and all because you've been resentful over my refusal to take you with me on some of my business trips."

A high-pitched trill of laughter erupted from her throat, but there was disparagement in her defiant gaze. "You arrogant ass."

With a distinct note of warning in his voice, he said, "This isn't getting us anywhere, Patricia."

Facing him with her hands on her hips, she cried, "And that's another thing. Do you realize that not once have you ever called me by my nickname, which you know I prefer?"

"Patricia is a beautiful name."

"It stinks," she retorted inelegantly.

In spite of himself, a tentative quirk of amusement quivered against one corner of his mouth. "Surely my name preference isn't the reason for our current... discord?"

"Don't be ridiculous."

Adding up each point on his fingers, he said, "Your name isn't at the root of your discontent, and nor is my leaving you on your own so frequently. For the life of me I've run out of ideas, so why don't you tell me what's really bothering you?"

"That's what's bothering me!"

When she pointed an accusing finger at him, his heavy black brows peaked upward in a startled arch, while his mouth compressed with visible impatience. "I beg your pardon?"

Glaring at him resentfully, she muttered, 'You're a cold man, Marcus Everett. A great big, oh, so polite, frozen Popsicle. You have all the pretentious, suave courtesies down to a science, but there's no real emotion behind your actions. You calculate each move you make, each word that comes out of your mouth, but in actuality you feel nothing. Not for yourself, or for me, and certainly not for our marriage.

"I've never been a real person to you," she concluded resentfully. "I hoped that by attempting to be the kind of wife you wanted me to be, eventually I could break through that armor you've surrounded yourself with. I thought we might grow closer. Instead I'm becoming nothing more than a reflection of your expectations, but I'm real, damn you! I have value in my own right, and not just as an ornament you delight in showing off. I'm losing myself, Marc, and I'm sick of the whole charade."

Marc stiffened at the implication behind that last remark, wondering if it was a roundabout way for Tricia to bring up the subject of a divorce. At the thought a surge of possessiveness rose up in him, and he quickly lowered his head to shield his expression from her discerning gaze. She belonged to him and always would, he raged inwardly, shocked to the back teeth by the primitive violence of his emotions.

Shifting his weight in the chair, he plucked a piece of lint from the knee of his cords with assumed casualness. His gaze remained fixed on the movement of his fingers, his voice carefully controlled, as he said, "Odd how this discontent erupted so suddenly, when I consider you married me knowing the responsibilities you would be assuming as my wife."

"But I didn't know my own personality would be stifled in the process," she cried. "I didn't know you would remain a frigidly contained, distant stranger."

"The way you talk, anyone would be forgiven for thinking me some kind of monster." He glanced at her as he uttered the deprecating remark, and then quickly averted his gaze once more. "I've always tried to behave toward you with gentleness and consideration, Patricia."

"Maybe your preoccupation with building an empire is part of the problem, have you ever thought of that? You are so much the socially conscious gentleman, you've forgotten who you really are. The true Marcus Everett is kept hidden behind a carefully devised facade, one even I am not supposed to question. Instead I'm expected to continue to follow the original script you provided me with, never changing or evolving into my full potential as an individual. But it's all pretense, can't you see that, Marc? A woman can't be satisfied with such a demoralizing scenario forever."

"Just what would it take to satisfy you?"

The softness of his voice was misleading, as Tricia discovered when she met his darkly speculative eyes. A maelstrom of emotion had built in their depths during the past several minutes, and now those sinfully black orbs were glittering with barely suppressed rage. The sight caused her stomach to churn with a nervousness that made her want to run screaming from the room.

Yet her relationship with her husband was too important for her to simply back away from this confrontation. She didn't want to be deliberately cruel, but if they couldn't learn to communicate with each other there wouldn't be a relationship. It was stagnating; dying from neglect. She had to do everything in her power to save her marriage, or spend the rest of her life wondering if she could have.

Inhaling deeply, she carefully formulated her next words in her mind. When she spoke, it was with a sad certainty, which lent poignancy to her voice. "Think me an idiot if you must, but I used to imagine that someday you would feel something more than pride of possession toward me, Marc."

Still not looking at her, he murmured, "Tell me something, Patricia. Is Donovan Lancaster, that scion of upper crust society, more your idea of what a gentleman should be?"

With a wry quirk to her lips, Tricia admitted, "I wondered if Martha had given you the name of my escort tonight. And to answer your question... yes, Donovan is every inch a gentleman."

Slowly smoothing a single finger from his knee to his thigh, he added, "And would you consider him more suitable husband material, my dear?"

Despite her attempt to control it, an irrepressible giggle tore from her throat. "Only if I've developed a fondness for cold fish, darling. The only thing that warms Donovan's heart is that shelter he operates for runaway teens."

His voice had grown quieter and more stilted as each minute passed, until it was no more than a thready rasp deep in his throat. But the eyes he'd lowered as he spoke were like burning coals when he lifted his head and fixed her with a basilisklike stare that caused her entire body to clench in sudden panic. "Maybe you have developed such tastes," he speculated harshly. "Tell me, Patricia, how does he rate as a lover? Do you respond to him with more enthusiasm than you do to me?"

Blind shock rendered her speechless for a moment, and then all hell broke loose. With a tormented cry she flew across the room, her control shattered in an instant. "How dare you?" she cried out, her hands clasping and unclasping impotently at her sides. "How dare you think that Donovan and I . . . that we're—"

"Lovers?" His lids narrowed broodingly, a flash of bitterness in the depths of his eyes. "Quite easily, I assure you."

"Dammit, Marcus, I'm not your mother!"

With a succinct curse he lunged forward and pulled her into his arms. She landed on top of him, the breath leaving her lungs in a startled expulsion as he demanded, "What in hell do you know about my mother?"

All color drained from her face, leaving it as white as an alabaster figurine as she lay sprawled between his splayed, muscular legs. The clamp of his powerful thighs stilled her struggles, which ceased abruptly when she felt his loins hardening in involuntary response against her quivering belly. As she tentatively braced her weight against his chest with both hands, she whispered, "Please, I didn't mean to . . ."

With grim persistence he cut her off, his expression boding ill for any attempt at subterfuge. "Answer me, Patricia!"

As she stared in horror at her husband, Tricia felt as though she'd opened Pandora's box. Tonight had been geared to gain Marc's attention, but she'd gotten more than she'd bargained for. Never had she seen such a look of unbridled emotion on his face, and nor had he ever touched her with anything but careful tenderness. Appalled at the result of her machinations, she breathlessly attempted to sooth the savage beast she'd so unwittingly aroused.

Three

Defensively spreading her fingers open against the front of Marc's shirt, Tricia felt her hands cushioned by the thick pelt of hair that covered most of his broad chest. Even through his clothing and the natural insulation created by his body, she could feel his furnacelike heat against her palms. At her touch his heart began pounding out an erratic rhythm, which exactly matched the increased cadence of her own. Her breath emerged from her parted lips in a futile series of choking gasps, and she hesitated long enough to regain a measure of calm before attempting to respond to his question.

When she could finally bring herself to speak, her eyes held a sheen of tears. "I—I know she left your father for another man when you were a boy," she said softly. "I-it must have hurt you terribly when she deserted you. You—you must have felt betrayed by one of the people you loved most in the world."

"Loved?"

Although momentarily distracted by a pair of drowned pansy eyes, the laugh he eventually uttered was harsh with derision. "I was hardly a boy at fifteen, and by the time she took off I was more than happy to see the last of her. My father was the only one who begged her to stay, but then he'd gotten used to begging."

She gasped, her eyes widening in disbelief. "Surely you don't mean that, Marc?"

"I can assure you I do," he asserted bitterly. "I was tired of watching my father try to hide his shame by drinking himself to death. A mining town tends to be insular, and at least with her gone the gossip stopped."

Tricia's face took on a grayish pallor. "I had no idea that your father was an alcoholic," she whispered brokenly. "I'm so sorry, Marc."

"And I regret that my revelations have shocked you," he informed her stiffly. "I just took it for granted that Martha would have mentioned Lydia's quaint little habit of playing the whore with any man that would have her. God knows, Martha has no reason to feel any loyalty toward my mother. The immoral witch tried to seduce Cully often enough."

Tricia had been staring at a point between his strong brown throat and his collarbone, but at his remark her head jerked upward until she could meet his stony-eyed gaze. Shocked to the core by his vicious denunciation of the woman who had given him life, she stammered, "P-please don't blame Martha for telling me the little she did, Marc. You know she cares for you too much to betray your confidence, but I was curious about your childhood. You've always refused to discuss your past with me, and Martha knew I was only trying to gain a little understanding of the man I married."

She moistened her drying lips nervously, and Marc's body stiffened with more than anger as his eyes followed the movements of that darting pink tongue. "Maybe it's more than understanding you want from me," he suggested tautly. "Have I been away from home too long, Patricia?"

Weeks of celibacy suddenly combined with his anger and resentment, and with a muttered growl his descending head blocked the light from his wife's eyes. Her head was forced back until her neck arched painfully, as his mouth collided with hers in a demand of unbridled possession. As his tongue thrust past the barrier of her even white teeth, his fingers began to trace her sensitive spinal column with probing insistence.

Then those demanding, caressing fingers moved even lower, until he was able to cup her rounded buttocks in both hands. As he pulled her tighter into the cradle of his thighs, he began grinding his hardening length against her corresponding softness with compulsive thoroughness. His breath heaving in and out of his chest like a bellows, he felt as though the top of his head was going to blow off. She was his wife, his whirling thoughts proclaimed, and he wanted her!

Tricia felt as though all the breath had been driven from her lungs. She was being stifled by his powerful body, her own hands helplessly trapped beneath his arms. Her fingers curled impotently around the thin material of his shirt, her fingernails inadvertently gouging his back. A muffled cry burst from Marc's throat as he felt those long, elegant nails dig into his flesh, and his entire body shivered in response.

Sensations she'd never experienced before ripped through Tricia, and she felt her own breath catch in amazement. The tiny sound that emerged from her parted lips served to increase her husband's mindless arousal, and his tongue began to thrust in and out of her mouth in a rhythm that matched his undulating hips. Dazed with disbelief and a wondrous sense of discovery, she eagerly spread open her hands and began to slide her palms over the rippling muscles of his back.

Instantly a melting heat began to spread inside her, dispelling her fear and pooling low in her belly until she began to tremble uncontrollably. It was a sensation she'd felt before, but never with such ferocity. She could feel her most sensitive flesh flowering open in unmistakable anticipation, and a low, throbbing pulse beat became synchronized with the flow of blood from her heart.

She was dizzy, disoriented, but gloriously, vividly alive! His desire for her was like a force too powerful to be contained, and it was feeding her starving senses until every nerve end in her body vibrated in response. With a sensation of utter abandon she pressed her moist palms against the curve of his spine, wishing there was no cotton barrier between them preventing the contact of skin on skin.

Once again her fingernails dug into him as she fought to contain her whirling senses, and a low, feverish moan whispered from her lips as she was bombarded with sensation after sensation. A feeling of elation swept through her, accompanied by an awareness of her own feminine power. She exulted in her ability to bring the man she loved to this level of arousal, her pleasure sweeter, knowing it was the first time he had ever lost his iron control with her. At long last he was man to her woman, with both of them locked in a sweet embrace as elemental as the ages.

As she felt his big body shaking against her in explosive desire, she began to understand the powerful lure of her own sexuality for the first time in her life. Tricia heard the rasp of her zipper as it was lowered, and she shivered with a delicious burst of excitement. She wanted to be naked in his arms, and the overpowering need she felt for his touch shocked her speechless.

"Patricia..."

Marc groaned her name like a man in torment, and every aroused inch of her body quivered at the sound.

His mouth opened against her neck, his tongue tasting her moistening flesh with a hunger he didn't try to restrain. She clutched at his shoulders as he bit down on the throbbing pulse he found there and began a rhythmic sucking.

The pain was a pleasure so great Tricia thought she would lose consciousness, especially when Marc tore open the back of her dress and thrust his hands against her naked back. Without hesitation his fingers slipped beneath the elastic waistband of her silky panties, his fingers flexing in synchronization with his devouring mouth. Tricia heard a low, keening cry vibrate in the air, only realizing that the sound was coming from her when she felt her husband's body clench and tauten.

Marc heard Tricia moaning with a sensation of horror, the red haze, which had distorted his thinking, lifting to reveal the savagery of his own actions. Tearing his mouth away from the perfumed softness of her slender neck, her stared down at the evidence of his passion in disbelief. Her flesh was damp from the glide of his tongue and mouth, but even now a reddening bruise was beginning to mar the perfection of her delicate white skin.

"Dear God, what am I doing?" The question reverberated endlessly in his brain, and was answered by the pressure and heat threatening to explode in his loins. Swallowing with difficulty, he recoiled from the certainty of what had nearly occurred in growing revulsion. He had almost raped his wife, he realized sickly, his self-disgust increasing when she looked up at him.

There was bewilderment and a questioning innocence in those beautiful blue eyes, and he thought he heard reproach in the sound of his name on her lips. "Marc?"

Lowering his lashes to shield his expression from her anxious gaze, he slid his hands over her arms until he clasped her face between his palms. He had regained a small amount of self-control, but he was all too aware that his passion was still red hot and ready to explode. "I think it's time you went upstairs," he ground out harshly.

"Upstairs?" she murmured, her thoughts disoriented. "But I . . ."

Pressing both thumbs against the softness of her trembling mouth, he shook his head. There was rejection in the dark eyes that studied her flushed features, and cool resolve in the voice that cut into her with the precision of a scalpel. "Our . . . discussion is at an end, Patricia. For God's sake, go to bed!"

His rejection a blow that shattered her budding self-confidence, she didn't struggle when he eased her into a sitting position on his lap. Instead she clutched the loosened folds of her dress so tightly her knuckles whitened, and rose slowly to her feet. Her dilated eyes reflected shame at her wanton behavior, and the anguished certainty that her actions had disgusted him.

Attempting to put her thoughts into words, she said, "I'm sorry I went to that stupid dinner party tonight,

Marc. I knew you'd be angry, but I...never meant this to happen. If I'd known about your mother, I never would have given you reason to question my loyalty by asking Donovan to be my escort.''

Her gentle apology did nothing to ease the guilt tearing him apart inside, especially when he knew the blame for what had just happened between them was his to bear. Tricia had a forgiving nature, but he wasn't so fortunate. He had subdued her anger in the basest way possible for a man to use against a woman, and it would be a long time before he would be able to forgive himself.

"If it means anything," he muttered tiredly, "my own behavior was way out of line. I never intended to use physical dominance as a weapon against you."

The brooding expression of self-contempt she saw on his face startled her, and made her ask herself if she had placed the wrong interpretation on his rejection of her. Could it be that it was himself he was disgusted with and not her? she wondered. Suddenly hopeful, she tried to reassure him in the most basic way possible. Hesitantly she lifted her hand and placed it gently against the rigid curve of his jaw.

Marc recoiled violently, and hope died in her breast as her hand fell to her side. The remaining flush of arousal drained from her cheeks and was replaced by a waxen pallor. "Why do you always shut me out?" she whispered plaintively.

A twin trail of tears began to trickle down her cheeks, and she closed her eyes to try to stem the flow.

As a result, she failed to see her husband wince as she asked, "Why do you lock yourself away in a place where I can't follow?"

Marc hovered on a razor edge, every instinct he possessed urging him to reach out and draw her along the path he'd just initiated. But he no longer trusted himself not to hurt her, and the knowledge struck at the pride he'd always had at his self-control. With calculated cruelty, he rasped harshly, "Because I don't want to be reached, my dear."

A sob caught in Tricia's throat as she absorbed the terrible truth behind his words, and with a strangled exclamation she turned and fled. She didn't see Marc lean forward and clutch his head in his hands. Nor did she hear the despairing cry he uttered as he listened to the sound of his wife running away from him in fear and disgust.

As silence descended on the room, Marc gave a cynical and totally unamused laugh. The horrified expression on Patricia's face just before she left haunted him, and he cursed himself for the bastard he was. He'd given her what she thought she wanted, and showed her a side of himself he had always kept hidden. He was truly his mother's son—the thought making him ill—the offspring of a woman who had given in to her sexual cravings and destroyed the one person who had loved her more than life.

Upstairs Tricia restlessly paced from one end of her cream and gold bedroom to the other. Even after taking a long, hot shower, her emotions were too turbulent to allow her to relax. She was still caught up in the brief magic of Marc's embrace, and she stared blindly at her surroundings as she tried to make sense out of what had happened downstairs. She remembered the raw power of the sexuality that had exploded between her and Marc, and her confusion deepened as responsive goose bumps popped out on her chilling skin.

Wishing she had chosen to put on something warmer after her shower than the thin, lacy nightgown she was wearing, she wrapped her arms across her chest and struggled to concentrate on familiar things. There on her oval mirrored dresser was the silver-plated comb and brush set her brother had bought her for her eighteenth birthday, and beside it was the milky glass atomizer of her favorite perfume.

With carefully measured footsteps she crossed the room, her bare feet sinking soundlessly into the plush carpeting. Lifting the flagon with a hand that shook visibly, she released the stopper and sniffed with closed eyes. The scent was soft and delicate and sweetly floral, and she suddenly found herself despising the contents. The perfume was as clean and simple and unsophisticated as she was, and was hardly likely to drive a man mad with passion. At least not her man, she decided with painful honesty.

What did she expect? she asked herself with justified cynicism. She'd known when he married her that Marc wasn't in love with her. He had made no secret of the fact that he viewed their relationship more in the nature of a partnership advantageous to them both. She would gain a wealthy, considerate husband, while he would acquire a wife with the social background he coveted. Thus the cold, calculated bargain had been struck, but she had been confident enough of her own feelings for him to take a chance on becoming his wife.

Unfortunately her confidence hadn't lasted much beyond the ceremony. Her shyness and the knowledge that he didn't love her had paralyzed her both in bed and out, and their honeymoon had largely been an exercise in disappointment for her and frustration for him. Neither of them had been reluctant to return home and take up their daily lives, and for a while she'd been relatively content.

But she'd expected more than a predictable routine and a comfortable life-style, she knew that now. Replacing the perfume on the corner of the French Provincial dresser where it belonged, she realized how big a mistake it had been to enter into a marriage thinking she could change Marc. She should have held out for a long engagement, and utilized that time in getting to know the man who had attracted her in ways she hadn't fully understood.

That's what Maria had advised, she remembered suddenly. Best friends since their senior year of high school, the other woman had known Marc since going to live with her foster father. When Thomas Phelps had died several years later of a massive coronary, Maria had been devastated. Marc had encouraged her to take a job managing the apartment complex where she lived, which was owned by his corporation, in an attempt to help her recover from her grief.

Marc's kindness to her friend had intrigued Tricia, especially since she knew of his reputation as a cold, ruthless businessman with little claim to benevolence. Her curiosity had grown to almost obsessive proportions after she saw a picture of him in the local newspaper, his dark good looks seeming to leap out of the pages of the *Daily Review* and straight into her dreams.

So when she phoned Maria one morning and was told that her boss was due to arrive shortly, Tricia hadn't let any grass grow under her feet. She'd dressed in a gold, elegantly cut two-piece ensemble, which she knew showed her tall, slim figure to its best advantage, and just happened to stop by Maria's office to ask her to lunch. As she had hoped, Marc had taken them both to eat, and from that afternoon on there had been no turning back.

Within two weeks she and Marc were engaged, and Maria hadn't hesitated to protest such haste. "You and Marc are still practically strangers," she reminded Tricia worriedly. "You're letting that impulsive streak of yours overrule common sense, Trish. At least give yourself a little time before you marry to get to know him."

"The way you and Drew have?" she'd retorted sarcastically. "I'd like to be married sometime in this century, thank you very much!"

Maria had paled at this snide reference to her on-going feud with Tricia's brother, which had begun almost from the moment they met. But she had stood her ground, insisting that there was no comparison between her relationship with Andrew Sinclair and Tricia's relationship with Marcus Everett. "I have no intention of marrying your blind, egotistical, infuriating brother, Tricia."

But knowing how much Maria loved Drew, no matter how she protested, had deafened Tricia to her advice. So she and Marc were pronounced man and wife in a hurried but grandiose wedding ceremony barely two months later. She'd been so certain of herself that day, she recalled wryly, so convinced that the solemn, reserved man who stood beside her would soon accept her into his heart as well as his home. God, how wrong she'd been!

With a sense of futility she turned abruptly, her glance encompassing pale gold walls, luxurious wall-to-wall carpeting, and a double-sized four-poster complete with a frilled, Laura Ashley floral print canopy cover and matching bedspread. Lace-trimmed, silk throw pillows piled against the headboard matched the off-white furniture, and the gold handles of a tallboy in the corner reflected the shadow of a slowly revolving fan inset into the ceiling.

The fan was embellished with tulip-shaped domes that muted the glare of the light bulbs hidden inside. Except for the back wall, which was constructed of glass and offered a splendid view of the well kept grounds, each of the other walls contained delicately carved doors. One led to the hallway, the other opened into an ensuite dressing area and bathroom, and a third linked her private space with Marc's via a large sitting room.

When she'd gone over the plans of the house with him, she had assumed that this space was intended to be a nursery. She laughed harshly, not at all amused at the memory. By the time she discovered differently, she remembered with cynical self-castigation, she'd been too embarrassed and intimidated by the reality of marriage to protest their separate sleeping arrangements.

Embarrassed and hurt, she recalled with a bitter twist to her lips. While they had been on their honeymoon Marc had given a team of interior decorators explicit instructions, and when they returned home she'd been presented with a *fait accompli*. Her husband had shown her all the amenities he'd provided for her comfort with a self-satisfied air, and she'd been installed here in isolated splendor ever since.

And she hated it! She hated the damn hothouse atmosphere; she hated the cold, lonely bed, and she especially hated the feeling that she was a prisoner in a luxurious cage. Her husband might revere his privacy, she thought indignantly, but she didn't necessarily have to follow suit. This might be the way Marc presumed the wealthy were supposed to live, but she wasn't buying it. She had grown up with two parents who loved each other, and being wealthy had never prevented them from sharing a bedroom.

With a muffled imprecation, Tricia wrenched the rose and gold flowered spread back, and folded it at the foot of the bed. At the moment all she wanted to do was crawl beneath her covers to hide, but she knew that was impossible. She couldn't escape her thoughts, or wipe away the feel of Marc's hands and mouth from her skin. She might cower in the dark and pretend that the scene downstairs had never occurred, but there was no way she was going to be able to prevent humiliation from eating into her soul like bitter acid.

Four

Tricia's eyes felt gritty from lack of sleep as she descended the stairs the next morning and headed toward the breakfast nook with a carefully measured tread. Just the thought of food made her stomach recoil in protest, but she didn't want Marc to think she was avoiding him. After what had happened between them last night they were on shaky enough ground emotionally, and she didn't want to add to the tension between them by appearing to sulk.

"Good morning," she greeted in subdued tones, eyeing his usual office attire with an apathetic lack of interest.

He glanced up at her from over the edge of the newspaper he held, his eyes inscrutable as he surveyed her crisply tailored cream pantsuit and yellow, ruffle-bodiced blouse. The color accentuated the delicate flush on her cheeks, and her hair framed her face in waves of gold. She'd never been more beautiful, he decided, unless he counted last night. His jaw clenched tightly at the memory.

Carefully controlling the increased cadence of his breathing, he complimented her on her appearance. "Thank you," she responded, her lashes flickering slightly as she sought to hide her surprise at his conciliatory attitude. She started to seat herself, before suddenly remembering that Martha had requested a few days off work. With a distracted glance at her watch, she asked, "What would you like for breakfast?"

Ignoring her question, he motioned toward a small box sitting on the table beside her plate with a negligent toss of his head. Early morning sunlight poured through the multipaned windows that bordered three sides of the breakfast nook, and the blue and silver foil paper covering the gift sparkled enticingly. "I thought you agreed to stop this habit," she muttered in choked disapproval.

"We discussed the matter, but I don't remember making any promises."

Considering the way she was eyeing his offering, as though she suspected it contained a poisonous snake, he maintained a cool composure that surprised him. "I enjoy buying you things, Patricia."

Deliberately averting her gaze from the object under discussion, she referred back to her earlier question. "What would you like to eat?"

The paper rustled loudly as he folded it and placed it beside his full coffee cup. Lifting the steamy beverage to his lips with a hand that appeared too large to safely handle the delicate china, he stared at her over the rim. "I'd planned on just having toast this morning. Why don't you sit down and open your present while I take care of kitchen duty. Would you like an egg with your toast?"

Trying not to shudder at the thought, she shook her head and seated herself before her wobbly legs had a chance to give out on her. "Just toast will be fine, thank you."

Once he left the room Tricia studied the perfectly arranged place settings, her mouth quirking in an unamused smile. Until now she hadn't realized Marc capable of such homey skills, which just went to prove how little she knew about the man she'd married. His pleasant attitude was also a surprise, but she wasn't about to question his demeanor. At least his anger of last evening hadn't carried over into today. Right now, she felt far too fragile to withstand another argument.

She also felt unable to cope with this newest sop to his conscience. With trembling hands she cradled her overly warm cheeks, and returned her attention to the foil-wrapped box awaiting her attention. She stared at it with loathing. It was just another consolation prize, she thought cynically, a reward for being a good little wife and not complaining about her husband's frequent absences from home. Well, she was going to start complaining... and loudly.

Marc didn't know her any better than she knew him, and it was her own fault. She had consciously subdued her own personality to meet Marc's requirements for a wife, but only because she'd been afraid of losing him. She was still afraid, she acknowledged with inner trepidation, but something had to be done. A marriage needed to be based on a firm foundation of mutual respect and love in order to succeed, and she was determined that their relationship was going to be given a fighting chance to survive!

She had started asserting herself in small ways at first, and had begun to despair of ever reaching his heart. To be honest, she'd begun to fear that he didn't have one to reach. Yet when he'd held her in his arms last night, she remembered with a shiver of response, she'd felt it nearly beating her to death. Now she was certain that there was an exciting, sensual male buried inside her husband's body, and she was going to bring him out if it was the last thing she did.

Tricia was sick of the sham her marriage had become. She was tired of cold consideration and empty lovemaking; she wanted heated passion and the fullness of love. She was tired of controlled responses and a restrained touch; she wanted wild emotion and mind-blowing desire. In effect, she wanted the total man and not just the courteous stranger who hid from her in the dark.

Pushing the unwanted gift aside, she grabbed her cup and stomped into the kitchen. She headed directly for the coffeepot, her mouth set in a petulant slant as she poured the aromatic beverage into her cup. Her stomach lurched protestingly as the steamy scent rose to her nostrils, but she ignored her body's reluctance to have any food or drink pass her lips. Sipping the drink gave her something to do with her hands, and provided a focus for her attention. At all costs, she needed to avoid looking at the dark-suited man standing beside the toaster.

"I was planning to bring the pot into the breakfast room," he informed her in amusement. "Couldn't wait for a caffeine jolt, huh?"

Resenting his disgustingly cheerful attitude, she glared at him. "I'm in a hurry to get to work. Don't bother with that toast."

"It's already done."

"I'll take a piece with me then."

Buttering a last slice of warm bread, he placed it on a platter holding several others and added marmalade to the tray. Ignoring the distinct note of truculence in her voice, he moved beside her and reached for the coffeepot. When the glass carafe was balanced to his satisfaction on the tray, he lifted his load and began to exit the room. "Come along, then. Everything's ready."

She followed him reluctantly, pausing beside the table when she noticed his gaze zero in on that damnably shining object beside her plate. "Aren't you going to open it?" he questioned quietly.

The softness of his voice caused the shorter hairs on the nape of her neck to prickle with alarm, and she knuckled under to the pressure of his unspoken disapproval like the coward she was. Tearing away the wrapping, she lifted the lid on the black velvet box and gasped at the contents. A pair of diamond earrings, each perfect in shape and size, winked up at her with a bluish white glow. "They're lovely," she remarked dully.

"I bought them to go with the bracelet I gave you last December," he replied with a complacency that grated on her already lacerated nerves. Remembering his conversation with Cully yesterday evening, his mellow tones slipped into clipped hardness. "Next time I visit Tiffany's, I'll bring you back a matching necklace."

Snapping the lid closed, she extended the box to him. "I don't want them, nor do I want a necklace to match!"

He slowly lowered the tray still clasped in his hands, and studied her frozen features without attempting to retrieve his gift. "You what?"

"I said I don't want them," she repeated, unconcerned with her rudeness as she replaced the box on the table.

"Don't be childish," he snapped, completely out of patience with her. "Is this some form of retaliation for last night?"

"Is it childish to expect something more from my husband than expensive trinkets he can well afford?" she ground out tearfully. "A little time and attention wouldn't come amiss, Marcus."

"Dammit, I'll take you with me the next time I go away on a business trip! Will that satisfy you?"

"You just don't understand, do you?" she whispered sadly. "I want to be with you, but not if it means having you resent my presence. A woman needs to know she's wanted, not just tolerated."

"The way Lancaster wants you?"

The ugly accusation hovered in the air between them, and Marc cursed himself for allowing the words to pass his lips. He was especially regretful when he saw the wounded look in his wife's eyes, and the visible trembling of her soft mouth. "I didn't mean that," he muttered stiffly, "but I'm not going to pretend that I approve of your friendship with another man. I don't want you seeing him again, Patricia."

"He's been like a brother to me—since childhood, and I refuse to allow you to destroy a relationship that means so much to me. God knows you control every other aspect of my life, but you can't dictate who I care about."

With a scowl, he ran an impatient hand over his hair, his dark eyes brooding as he studied her pinched and defensive features. "My wishes don't matter to you?"

"They matter," she replied, her eyes filling with tears. "They matter more than you know, and possibly more than you deserve."

With that she turned and walked away from him, her posture eloquent with dignity and pride.

Tricia was never more glad to reach her office than she was that morning, but after her nine o'clock appointment left, she felt the walls closing in on her. Everywhere she looked, from the softly muted landscapes on the walls to the oak cabinet in the corner, she was reminded of Marc. He'd surprised her with the pictures on the day her office furniture was delivered, and the hand-tooled cabinet had replaced the ugly metal monster she'd originally ordered.

Even the plush burgundy carpet had been his idea. She had been satisfied with the original, but he had taken an aversion to the thin, serviceable brown floor covering. Marc didn't like brown, which was why she never wore it. As usual she'd let him have his way, and at the thought she tilted her rounded chin to a belligerent angle. Although he didn't know it yet, those days were gone. Especially after their most recent contretemps.

She was no longer satisfied to meekly sit back and take the line of least resistance. A mischievous smile suddenly softened the compressed line of her lips as she glanced at the gold bangle watch on her wrist. Yes, there was just enough time if she hurried, she decided. Pushing herself away from her hideously expensive desk, another gift from Marc, she rose to her feet.

Tricia grabbed her purse from the top desk drawer, a low trill of laughter escaping her mouth. As a psychologist, it was about time she started following the advice she so often gave her patients. Sitting around here moping and soul-searching wasn't doing her a bit of good, and it was past time that she did something to cheer herself up. Her eleven o'clock appointment had called to cancel, and she didn't have another patient scheduled until late afternoon.

She was still meeting Donovan for lunch at twelve-thirty, although after her latest argument with Marc she'd been tempted to call and cancel. But she'd stood firm in her determination to preserve her friendship with the other man, and now she was glad she had. Southland Mall was practically around the corner from the restaurant she and Donovan had agreed on for lunch, and she was suddenly in a mood to splurge!

Her face glowed above the yellow silk blouse and cream pantsuit Marc had complimented her on this morning, and as she burst through her door with renewed vigor her receptionist responded to her smile with genuine fondness. "You certainly seem brighter than you did an hour ago," she informed her boss in affectionate tones.

Pressing a silencing finger to her lips, Tricia whispered, "That's because I just thought of the perfect way to cheer myself up. I'm going to play hooky and go shopping for a new dress. Will you cover my tracks, Eddy?''

The older woman would have done anything for the slender imp grinning at her with such an irrepressible gleam in her blue eyes. Having topped the fifty mark when she found herself divorced and in strained circumstances, Edna Carruthers had taken a secretarial refresher course and had begun job hunting after an absence from the job force of nearly twenty-five years.

After being repeatedly turned down because she was ''over qualified,'' a polite and legally acceptable term for ''too old,'' or because she didn't have computer training, she'd been at the end of her rope when she answered Patricia Everett's ad in the paper. She'd explained her current situation and her qualifications almost by rote, certain she was wasting her time even applying for the position of receptionist.

Yet after less than fifteen minutes a soft voice asked, ''Would you be willing to combine the duties of a receptionist with those of a secretary, at least until my patient files are healthier?''

Edna hadn't hesitated to reply in firm yet rather shaken tones. ''Certainly, Mrs. Everett!''

Her new employer had simply grinned, and said, ''You only have to call me Mrs. Everett when we want to impress someone with our professionalism. When we're alone, call me Tricia.''

Then she'd frowned, and tilted her head to one side in a questioning attitude. "You don't mind if I call you Eddy, do you?"

Not waiting for an answer to her inquiry, twin dimples had peeped out beside each corner of Tricia's mouth as she explained, "You have such kind brown eyes and a lovely smile. Edna sounds so staid and starchy, just like Patricia. I hate formality."

From that moment on Eddy, as she'd been dubbed, became Tricia Everett's most devoted follower. Now, as she glanced around the empty reception area, she responded to her employer's earlier question with a smiling air of conspiracy. "I'll do my duty or die trying, boss. I'll man the phones, barricade the doors, and throw anyone who asks for you off the scent. Nobody is going to come up on you from behind while I'm on the job!"

Tricia saluted smartly. "I knew I could count on you, general."

Edna nodded, but a sudden thought caused her forehead to wrinkle in puzzled conjecture. "You hate shopping for clothes. How is that going to cheer you up?"

Tricia's eyes sparkled with suppressed mirth. "This time I have a specific goal in mind, a brown dress I spotted in a window display last week."

It was obvious from her expression that Edna had drawn a blank, and Tricia explained gaily, "Marc detests brown."

"Ah," the other woman murmured sagely. "Is this all out war or another skirmish?"

Tricia's eyes narrowed as she contemplated the question. "I think I've declared war, Eddy," she stated softly. "As I once told my sister-in-law, I'm going to rattle that man's bones."

"Oh, it's a good thing you mentioned Mrs. Sinclair," Edna exclaimed, rushing to her desk and returning with a note clutched in her hand. "She phoned while you were seeing Mr. Palmer, but told me not to interrupt your session. She wanted to invite you to her house for an impromptu barbecue tomorrow afternoon."

"Maria's parties are always impromptu," Tricia retorted. "She's another advocate of informality. Says an unplanned get-together is always more fun."

Appearing momentarily flustered, Edna said, "She invited me to come, but I don't know if I should."

Tricia's brows peaked in a little frown. "Why ever not?"

"Well, I am just your receptionist, Tricia. I'm certain Mrs. Sinclair only invited me for politeness' sake."

"You're more than a secretary, you're my friend," Tricia retorted in a no-nonsense manner. "And Maria's no fool. She tasted those double-fudge brownies you made last Christmas, and I bet she suggested you bring a couple of dozen with you, didn't she?"

Edna's mouth flew open in amazement. "How did you know?"

Tricia laughed and tapped her temple sagely. "Madame E sees all and knows all. Anyway," she continued in a normal voice, "all Maria's friends are used to providing their own goodies at one of her spur-of-the-moment gatherings. Since most of her free time is taken up with her volunteer work at the Family Assistance Center for Emergency Shelter, we'd all starve if we didn't."

Laughing, Edna suggested she make up a quadruple batch of brownies. Nodding in agreement, Tricia asked, "Did Maria mention anything else she wanted?"

"Only to know if Mr. Everett... ah... I think she said 'threw a fit' last night when you weren't there to greet him in the traditional manner."

"Why do you think I'm buying the brown dress, Eddy?"

The office door closed behind her, and even after Tricia had reached the elevator she could still hear her friend's laughter.

Donovan Lancaster was an easy man to spot, even in a crowd. His thick, dark blond hair was overly long, and the twin slashes of white at his temples added distinction to the informal style. His manner and choice of clothing was usually as casual as his haircut, but Tricia knew this laid-back impression was deceptive. In actuality Donovan was always poised on a knife edge, his special forces training and active duty in

Vietnam having left him with a survival instinct most men never have to acquire.

His craggy, broad features and thin-lipped mouth attested to every one of his forty-one years, as did the lines that fanned out beside his odd-colored eyes. They were a deep, darkly golden brown in hue, with an intriguing slant at each corner. In fact his kids, as he referred to the teens who found shelter beneath his roof, referred to him as "The Lion," but not usually to his face. They were too proud of his insistence that they use his first name to call him anything but Donovan.

When Tricia reached the corner table Donovan had appropriated for them, he rose to his full height to greet her. As he pulled out a chair for her, with the suave manners that had been drummed into him from birth, she found herself thinking how well his nickname suited him. He moved with the sinuous grace of a big, rangy jungle beast, his lean, muscular body controlled and powerful.

But unlike his kids, Tricia never hesitated to tease him whenever the opportunity presented itself. Shaking a white linen napkin into her lap, she grinned and greeted him with the irreverence of a long-time friend. "Hi, you gorgeous animal, you. Why am I being treated to lunch, or do you want me to make a guess?"

Returning to his seat, he lowered his body into his chair with languid ease. A wry quirk indented one corner of his mouth, and he studied Tricia's animated features with habitual intensity. "Think you know me so well, do you?"

Taking the chiding question seriously, she cocked her head to one side and contemplatively surveyed him for several moments. "You never let anyone get close enough to know you, Donovan," she replied gently. "Unlike the lion, you choose to walk alone."

Two formidably bushy eyebrows rose, and a rare smile appeared to lighten his somber countenance at this allusion to his infamous sobriquet. "Alone, with upward to forty kids housed at my estate?"

"There's safety in numbers."

Grabbing a bread stick from a woven basket placed in the center of the linen-draped table, he bit into it with a crunch of strong white teeth. Chewing slowly, he nodded in her direction. "Got it in one, Bubbles."

Tricia groaned at the sound of her own childhood label, but was forced to stifle her instinctive retort. A gray-and-white-uniformed waitress had approached their table, her manner preoccupied as she took their orders. After her somewhat harried departure, Tricia fixed the man seated across from her with a reproving glare. "I finally got Drew to stop calling me by that repulsive name, but you've always been a tougher prospect than my brother."

Finishing off his bread stick with evident enjoyment, he laughed, albeit with rusty huskiness, at her indignant expression. "At seventeen he still had you firmly placed on that pedestal, but I was older than Drew by a good five years. I recognized a budding blackmailer when I saw one."

Tricia widened her eyes, her expression unbelievably innocent. "I only happened to tell him that I thought he should introduce Mother to his newest girlfriend. You remember, that busty brunette who moved into the Culpepper's guest cottage the summer before you left for Vietnam?"

"That brunette was all of twenty-five, divorced, and inordinately fond of younger men. Drew almost died when he caught you spying on them."

Her disdainful expression was ruined by a giggle. "I just happened to be riding my bike past her yard."

Donovan snorted. "Yeah, after following him for over half a mile to play nosey parker."

"Could I help it if there was a big round knothole in the woman's fence?"

"Luckily it was big enough for Drew to spot you, or you would have really gotten an eyeful."

"I did anyway," she admitted with a grin. "The first thing Drew did when they jumped into her pool was to make a grab for the strings of her bikini top. Although," she interjected primly, "she was falling out of the thing anyway."

"I opted for spanking your bottom when Drew told me what you'd done, but my friend was made of weaker stuff," Donovan informed her wryly. "He was too afraid you'd go screaming bloody murder to your folks."

"Mother would have had spasms." Silence reigned for a moment as she remembered all the ice cream sundaes she'd coaxed from her brother after that incident. "Not only was Drew under eighteen, but she had his virginal status firmly fixed in her mind."

Resting her elbows on the table, she cupped her chin in her hands and leaned forward confidingly. Although she managed to keep a serious demeanor, her eyes sparkled wickedly. "Was he still a virgin?"

Donovan was saved from a reply by the arrival of their lunch, and the next several minutes passed with desultory conversation. But as soon as the edge was taken off of their appetites, Donovan returned to the subject of his friend. "How are Drew and Maria doing these days? I haven't seen them since the wedding."

"You wouldn't have seen them then if you hadn't been roped into being my brother's best man," she chided gently. "You and Drew were always together when you were younger."

His mouth quirked wryly. "He started following me around about the time you were born, and I was never able to shake him off."

"He did have a gigantic case of hero worship," she admitted quietly, "but you know you enjoyed playing big brother. That's why it's hard to accept the distance that's grown between you over the years. You rarely see each other now."

"My fault," he remarked stiffly. "Too much exposure to wedded bliss gives me hives."

"And too much work is going to give you rigor mortis, my friend."

A spark of amusement deepened the gold in his eyes. "That isn't what your father used to tell me!"

"Yes," she agreed with a burst of laughter. "Daddy used to froth at the mouth when you assured him you wanted to be a rich playboy when you graduated from high school. When you enrolled in college I think he got down on his knees to give thanks." She hesitated, and added, "I know he did when you returned safely from Vietnam."

A brooding light entered his eyes. "At least he gave a damn. Your parents were the only ones who ever did."

Donovan hadn't been as fortunate with his own parents, Tricia remembered, which was why he'd spent so much time at their house during his youth. His mother and father had been jet-setters, rarely home and indifferent to their son when they were. He'd spent most of his childhood on his grandfather's estate, alone except for the paid staff and the elderly gentleman who had usually been too ill to provide much companionship for a lonely little boy.

Donovan was reaching for another bread stick, and on impulse Tricia leaned forward and placed her hand over his. "We all loved you, Donovan."

"Which is why I didn't follow the devil's path straight to hell," he admitted gently.

They shared a quiet moment of understanding, their gazes locked together and their hands touching across the distance that separated them. Then Donovan shrugged off his introspective mood, and slouched against the back of his chair. "I wonder where that waitress got to? I'd like another cup of coffee."

Tricia turned her head to glance around the room, and her gaze collided with a pair of flashing black eyes set in a face as hard and cold as chiseled rock. "Uh-oh," she muttered in dismay.

When she'd agreed to meet Donovan here, she'd forgotten that this restaurant was only a few blocks from her husband's office building. And if Marc's expression was anything to go by, that oversight had just landed her in some very hot water. As if she wasn't already in enough after last night and this morning, she thought, suppressing a cowardly urge to dive under the table.

Donovan's gaze swiveled in the direction she was staring, and a curious look of satisfaction crossed his mobile features. "Jealousy is a terrific motivator, Bubbles. Want me to jump up and plant a juicy kiss on your homely mug?"

"Don't you dare," she whispered.

"You've been married to that ice sculpture for over a year," he murmured. "Isn't it time you thawed him a bit?"

"I'm working on it," she snapped. "But thawing him is one thing, turning him into a homicidal maniac is quite another."

"From the look of things you've succeeded at both," he remarked, lazily watching as Tricia's husband began to head for their table. "I'd certainly enjoy helping you speed up the process, which was why

I agreed to escort you to that boring dinner party last night. It was also why I helped you kill time until you were good and late getting home. You know I never approved of your marriage to Everett."

"Will you please behave yourself?" she pleaded nervously.

He wiped his mouth and threw his napkin down beside his plate. "You're really crazy about that gold-plated calculator, aren't you?"

Praying that Donovan wouldn't taunt Marc into losing his temper, her voice held a plaintive note of which she was unaware. "Stop insulting him," she whispered. "And yes, I love my husband very much."

With an aggravatingly conspiratorial grin, Donovan replied, "Then have at 'em, Bubbles. If his expression is anything to judge by, you've already got him on his ear."

"Is this a private party, or can anyone join?" an all too familiar voice grated from right beside her.

Peeking up at the tall man through her lashes, Tricia smiled and swallowed uneasily. "Donovan and I had some business to discuss."

"So I saw," Marc responded coldly. "I walked here from my office. If your business is concluded, you can drive me back, my dear."

There it was, that dreaded "my dear," she thought, wondering how two simple words could send a zillion chills twanging up her spine. "You . . ."

Tricia cleared her throat and summoned up a weak protest. "But you haven't had lunch yet, Marc. Sit down and I'll flag the waitress. Donovan was just leaving, weren't you, Donovan?"

When Donovan nodded agreeably, Marc merely glared at him. In a voice cold enough to freeze the nose off a polar bear, he said, "It's too crowded in here and I'm a bit pressed for time, Patricia. I'll order something sent up from the executive dining room later."

Deciding against asking him why he hadn't done that in the first place if he was so pressed for time, she got to her feet with a semblance of calm she certainly didn't feel. "Sorry we didn't get around to that matter you wanted to discuss with me, Donovan. I'll call you at home sometime this weekend."

"Like hell you will," Marc muttered against her ear.

Observing the other man's reaction with every evidence of pleasure, Donovan shrugged dismissingly. "No sweat, sweetness."

Tricia scowled at him, and Marc's teeth ground together at the endearment. As he led his wife from the room, a husky laugh sounded from behind them as a pair of golden eyes followed their progress to the door. "You've got your tiger by the tail, Bubbles," Donovan mused thoughtfully. "I only hope you know what to do with him now."

Five

The Everetts maintained a strained silence as they traveled the short distance to Marc's office complex. He kept his eyes glued to the road, while Tricia apparently found much to fascinate her in the passing scenery. Marc had opted to drive his wife's flaming red Corvette with arrogant assumption, but for once Tricia hadn't uttered a word of protest at his high-handedness. She had simply glanced at him with an unusual degree of cynicism, and gracefully entered her car on the passenger side.

As he negotiated the heavy lunchtime traffic, Marc felt the responsive surge of power beneath his foot with increased aggravation. This was too damn much car for her to handle, he thought, but had he been able to make her see that? Oh, no! The stubborn woman had resented his attempt to convince her to be sensible. Come to that, he hadn't been successful at convincing her of much of anything lately.

She had traded in her old blue Datsun and bought the Corvette while he was checking out some property in Seattle. He'd been certain her timing was carefully calculated, because she'd known darned good and well that he would never have approved the purchase. He hadn't, he recalled angrily, and had immediately demanded that the car be returned to the dealer. There was too much power under the fiberglass hood for him to be comfortable with her driving it, but she hadn't viewed his disapproval as a natural concern for her safety.

Instead she had immediately taken umbrage, her blue eyes flashing as she calmly but firmly informed him that she would do no such thing. She loved her Corvette, she informed him, and she was an excellent driver. "I don't plan to push it flat out on the freeway, Marc."

He'd then argued in favor of something a little more sedate, and she had gone off like an exploding firecracker. "A little more suitable to my image as your wife, don't you mean?"

Unfortunately the control he'd been maintaining over his temper had slipped a notch, and he'd foolishly agreed with her. "A BMW or Mercedes would have been a more practical investment."

"Maybe I'm tired of being practical," she retorted with angry persistence. "After all, you're practical enough for both of us."

As was usual during any of their arguments, as soon as a personal note entered the conversation they both retreated from the fray. Marc hadn't mentioned the car again, and Tricia had continued to drive it. But now a pattern was beginning to emerge from his wife's first tentative rebellion against his wishes, and it was one with which he was far from comfortable.

Marc no longer felt as though he knew the woman he'd married. His calm, gentle-natured wife had metamorphosed into a female with an amazingly vivid personality and an even stronger will. She'd always been bright and beautiful, with a natural, inbred confidence he admired, but her recent behavior was something else again. Now she was stubborn, recalcitrant, irritating, and...exciting. This last admission caused his body to tighten responsively, and increased his irritation with himself as well as with her.

The steering wheel responded to the merest touch of his fingers as he swung into the Everett Property Management and Development Corporation's parking lot, but the sight of the four-storied, steel and tinted glass structure provided him with none of his usual satisfaction. He was too preoccupied with the woman seated beside him, his thoughts centered on her to the exclusion of everything else.

He'd been home less than twenty-four hours, he realized in growing confusion, and already she was driving him crazy. Always before he'd been the one to set the parameters in his relationships with women, but this female wasn't content to let him call the shots. Inch by inch she was infiltrating areas of his life he'd always held sacrosanct, and that knowledge made him extremely uncomfortable.

Her defiant attitude was disturbing the even tenor of his existence as nothing else could have, but it was something with which he was going to have to come to terms. Last night when she wasn't home to greet him, the sense of disappointment he'd experienced had shocked him. He had suddenly become aware of how dependent he was becoming on her, and that particular insight had caused a large portion of his anger toward her to become self-directed.

He had sat in the library waiting for her in brooding silence, intensely aware of his own isolation. Even the atmosphere of the house had been different without her in it, he thought, and the sense of homecoming he generally experienced upon his return from one of his business trips had been sadly lacking. It had set him to considering their relationship with more than a cursory attention to detail, and he hadn't liked the conclusions he'd drawn.

Before his marriage he'd often been alone, but he wasn't the kind of man who ever admitted to loneliness. If he'd sometimes felt as if something was missing from his life, he had quickly suppressed such thoughts. He'd told himself that his career was too all-encompassing; his independence too valued and rigidly maintained for that kind of weakness.

And he'd believed in his autonomy. At least he had until last night. A frown wrinkled his forehead at the grudging admission, and he surreptitiously glanced at his wife out of the corner of his eye. Immediately his breath became suspended in his lungs, and his hands tightened around the steering wheel as he absorbed the sunlit loveliness of her features.

Her profile was pure perfection, he decided thoughtfully, even with that pertly rounded chin of hers slightly raised in unconscious defiance. He smiled slightly as he admired the innate pride in her posture. Her complexion was as smooth and unflawed as a porcelain figurine, her nose straight and narrow, and the pouty fullness of her mouth seemed to be poised for a man's kiss.

Marc's heart began pounding so rapidly he felt in imminent danger of suffocation, and tiny beads of moisture began to form against his upper lip. Hellfire! he thought in self-disgust. He hadn't allowed his glance to fall below the damned woman's neck, and yet she already had him shaking like an adolescent with overactive hormones. His hands clenched and unclenched the sweat-moistened leather covering the steering wheel.

As he fought to regain his breath, he found himself wondering what in heaven's name was happening to him. He'd never felt so lacking in confidence with a woman, and the fact that he was married to this one only made that certainty more difficult to understand. If he discounted the last few months, he and his wife had lived together in what he'd always thought of as perfect harmony.

Only now he was being forced to face a few home truths, and he was just beginning to acknowledge what a smugly complacent idiot he'd been. His marriage had been slotted to fit into his schedule, but he'd never attempted to alter his life-style to suit his marriage. No wonder Patricia was in a state of rebellion, he decided bitterly, thoroughly disgusted with the image of himself as a mini-dictator that was forming in his mind.

She'd been right to accuse him of suppressing her personality for selfish reasons, but he honestly hadn't been aware of what he was doing. He wasn't used to sharing himself with anyone else, and had never considered the possibility that she might feel slighted by the omission. He hadn't even wanted her to resume her career after they were married, he remembered, but now he understood why she'd been so insistent. Why shouldn't she, when she'd been made to feel like a second-class citizen in her own home?

And the trouble was, he didn't know how to untangle the treads of their relationship. Hell, what did he know about being a husband? The only example he'd had was distorted by his father's alcoholism, and his parents' marriage certainly wasn't the kind of example he wanted to emulate. Just the memory of the abuse they'd so often hurled at each other caused him to cringe inwardly with revulsion, and reaffirm his vow that no woman would ever have that kind of hold over him.

With a muttered imprecation and an irritable twist of his wrist, Marc turned the key in the ignition to the off position. Immediately the roar of the Corvette's engine was subdued, and only the tinkling of the other keys on the ring managed to infiltrate the silence lingering between him and his wife. It was a silence born of discord, and he suddenly longed to end it with an apology.

The thought caused him to stiffen with instinctive rejection. He was damned if he was going to beg for smiles and crumbs of affection from anyone, let alone his own wife. He wasn't a weak, sniveling excuse for a man who needed a woman's approval to survive. A remembered voice from the past rose again in his mind, the piercing tones a whining entreaty, the anguished words slurred as he pleaded . . .

Grinding his teeth together, Marc tore the keys from the ignition and automatically deposited them in his breast pocket. As he turned to open the car door, a hand on his jacket sleeve delayed his progress. "May I have my keys, Marc?"

Ignoring the request, he thrust the door open and swung his long legs onto the ground. "You won't be needing them for a while," he stated abruptly.

"I'm seeing a patient for a therapy session at three o'clock," Tricia argued with as much patience as she could contrive under the circumstances.

"Call your receptionist and have her cancel it for you."

He got to his feet as he uttered the demand, and failed to see the expression on Tricia's face. With a strangled gasp she shot out of the passenger side like a rocket, and glared at him over the gleaming bonnet. "There's no way I can just cancel an appointment at the last minute. I have a responsibility to my patient."

Circling the vehicle without the slightest hesitation, Marc gripped her arm and began guiding her toward the building ahead of them. "You have a responsibility to me."

"Bull feathers," she muttered truculently.

Completely exasperated at her stubbornness, he said, "We need to get a few things straightened out regarding our opposing views of marriage, Patricia. I'm sorry, but I'm not prepared to wait for your convenience, my dear."

Halting with an abruptness that caused Marc to stumble, Tricia fixed him with a look sour enough to curdle milk. "If you call me that again, Marcus, I just might start screaming and never stop!"

As he righted himself, he wondered how he could ever have thought her cool and emotionless. Her cheeks were flushed, her eyes leaping with emotional fervor as she stared him down. As he inspected her passionately aroused features, he felt as though his mouth was stuffed full of cotton batting.

The way she was looking at him, it was obvious she thought it was his brain that was stuffed. "Are you just going to stand there and stare at me for the rest of the afternoon?" she added in frustration.

His tongue seemed to have thickened from a lack of moisture, preventing the words he wanted to speak from passing the tight line of his lips. Which was probably fortunate under the circumstances, he thought, bewildered by the full extent of the tension that was suddenly gripping his body in a cramping vise.

Marc felt confusion block his thinking processes. He wanted to grab hold of his wife and shake her silly. Then he wanted to... To what? he asked himself uneasily. This entire situation was obviously getting out of hand, and he feared he wasn't quite functioning with his usual level of calm competence.

In fact, far from it! His breathing was labored, his skin prickled, and his hands were sweaty. Just like the green kid he'd earlier likened himself to, he decided in disgust, and yet his resentment surprisingly gave way to humor when he managed to gather his thoughts and again focus his full attention on his wife.

She was gloriously aroused, all rosy cheeks and clenched fists and spitting, indignant eyes. The sun seemed to strike sparks off of the hair that waved around her delicately shaped skull, and he had the strongest urge to kiss away the scowl from her pouting mouth.

Marc was immediately able to imagine what would happen if he did, and it was a real struggle to keep his betrayingly twitching lips from exploding into a full grin. A series of slow, inwardly drawn breaths aided him in maintaining his self-control, and when he responded to her threat his voice was satisfactorily bland.

"If I call you what?" he asked, alluding to her earlier warning with deliberate provocation. "You really should be more precise when you threaten a man, my dear."

"That does it!" she raged.

Tricia's mouth flew open, but she never got a chance to make another sound. There in the middle of the parking lot, in full view of his office staff and anyone else who might pass by, her very proper, correct, conventional husband yanked her into his arms and covered her mouth in a kiss to rival the one he'd given her the night before. Her lips parted on a shocked gasp, and a hot, aggressive tongue thrust through the opening she'd unwittingly provided.

She did not react at all in the way he expected. Her knees sagged as her hands rose to clutch at his shoulders, her head spinning as the kiss deepened into a passionate assault that sizzled her brain. Excitement raced through her veins in a quicksilver flood, spreading a delicious heat through every inch of her body. Her nipples tightened at the crush of his chest against her tender breasts, and she found herself aching for the feel of his warm skin against her own.

The material of his suit jacket felt rough beneath her palms, and with mindless hunger her hands slid over his shoulders and wrapped themselves around his strong neck. Her fingers widened and speared into his thick hair, and shaped the angle of his head in silent encouragement.

The action resulted in a low groan that tore out of Marc's throat in a paean of arousal. She swallowed the sound along with the last of his breath, and yet he couldn't force himself to relinquish the sweetness of her mouth. His lips slanted over hers, twisting back and forth in a sensual rocking motion that increased the urgency of the kiss until they were both moaning their pleasure aloud.

A horn blared suddenly, and a raucous voice cried, "Way to go, man!"

Both Tricia and Marc stiffened, and jerked apart with self-conscious haste. He glanced at a freckle-faced teenager in a souped-up Chevy, who gunned his engine and rounded the corner on two wheels. "Dumb little jerk needs driving lessons," he muttered.

The prosaic judgment made Tricia laugh, and her eyes sparkled as she glanced up at him. "And we need pedestrian lessons," she teased. "Imagine an old married couple like us making out on a public street. We could have caused a major traffic jam."

Mesmerized by that fun-loving glint set into a breathlessly blue, crystalline background, Marc held her gaze as he brushed a probing finger over her kiss-moistened mouth. "Let's go," he urged huskily. "My office will provide us with all the privacy we need."

Her lashes rose with a flutter, while nervous tremors feathered her skin. Yet an impish impulse caused her to whisper, "Is there a lock on the door?"

She heard the rasping hiss of his breath with satisfaction, which increased a thousandfold at the darkening glance he speared her with. "You know damn well there is."

Actually she didn't, and at the realization her gaze fell to the center of his tie. She studied the swirling blue and gray pattern blindly for a moment, before putting her thoughts into words. "You've never invited me to visit you at your office."

"I've never . . . ?"

He paused as he absorbed the truth from her in stunned surprise, and immediately sought to lessen the guilt that assailed him at her reminder. "Since when does my wife need an invitation?" he questioned, his voice more defensive than he'd intended it to be.

"Since you went to great lengths to make her feel she wasn't welcome," she countered instantly. "You've always made it clear that your workplace is sacrosanct, Marc."

He had, but he didn't like hearing her say it. With a gesture of frustration he ran his hand over his hair, and said, "All right, I'm guilty as charged. Does that confession make you feel any better? If so, I'm 'inviting' you into my office right now, Mrs. Everett."

The harshness of his low tones altered from defensive accusation to a sensual growl, which caused a ripple of wild sensation to race down her spine. But it also served to raise her defensive radar. Thanks to her regrettable temper, Marc now had more than talking on his mind. So did she, she admitted with intrinsic honesty, but that didn't mean the time was right.

She thought of the wickedly sexy dress sheathed in plastic that was currently residing in the trunk of her car. She would put it on for him tonight, and knock his socks off. They would dine by candlelight, she decided dreamily, and he would be utterly fascinated by her witty....

Marc had a council meeting to attend tonight! Remembering such a mundane fact really put a crimp in her plans for a romantic evening, but if she kept her wits about her now she could probably manage to hold him off for another day. She hadn't spent the last few months studying a book on *How to Become a Sensuous Woman* for nothing, she reminded herself, and she certainly didn't feel ready to leap from Chapter One to Chapter Ten in a single afternoon!

Six

Especially not when there was still so much uncertainty marring her relationship with her husband, Tricia thought. Although saddened by the realization, she now felt hopeful that the barriers between them could eventually be torn down. Surely Marc wouldn't be exhibiting all the symptoms of extreme jealousy unless he cared for her?

Her weakening resolve was bolstered by that thought, and she reaffirmed that now was definitely not the time to act on impulse. Once his sexual urge was satisfied, Marc was going to remember why he'd been angry enough to practically drag her out of the restaurant. His disapproval over her friendship with Donovan would once again be at the forefront of his mind, and another argument would almost certainly ensue. Hardly a romantic prospect, she decided wryly.

And she wanted romance, she realized suddenly. She wanted soft lights and whispered words and a body aching for hers, which she wouldn't have if she succumbed to his desire for her now. He was a normal, healthy man, and he had been away from home for weeks. Right now she knew he needed the release, however temperate, her body had always provided for him upon his return. A little more frustration, she mused wickedly, combined with a shimmery cinnamon dress with no back and a neckline that plunged to her navel, and she would stand a much better chance of gaining her objective.

They had almost reached the edge of the parking lot, and Marc's arm circled her waist as he guided her onto the sidewalk fronting the street. His fingers flexed against her hip, and an unmistakable tremor of desire shot through her body. Suddenly afraid he might guess the reason why she'd begun trembling, she flinched away from him with undue haste.

"What's the matter?" he queried with an impatient frown.

Pausing in front of him on the sidewalk, she nervously studied his unyielding features and blurted out the first thought to enter her head. "This is not a good idea," she stated.

"What isn't?"

"Our, um... being together right now."

One corner of his mouth quirked at her dithering response, and a devilish glint appeared in his eyes. "Why, because we've never made love during the day before?"

Tricia shifted her weight from one foot to the other, unconsciously wincing when the toe of a horrendously expensive leather pump scraped against the sidewalk. "Because you're angry with me."

At the reminder, his mouth twisted with derisive cynicism. "You might say that."

"Then why are you . . . why are we . . . ?"

"Why are we heading for my office to indulge in a little afternoon delight?" he questioned mockingly. "Because it's closer than home, and I'm a bit. . .eager to settle our differences."

Annoyed at his trite description, she gritted her teeth and boldly met his eyes. "That isn't the reason you brought me here, Marc."

He tilted his head to one side, his gaze narrowing on her mutinous features. "Then what is?"

Although she tried to answer him with cool self-assurance, her voice quivered slightly. "You want to punish me."

Something shadowed and dangerous leaped to life in his eyes, and a scowl settled heavily on his features. "For God's sake, don't look at me like that!"

Her body jerked in surprise. "Like what?"

"As if you're afraid of me."

Both his voice and his expression were accusing, and her hands clenched into impotent fists at her sides. "Then stop glaring at me!"

He lifted his face toward the heavens as though seeking divine counsel, and rubbed the back of his neck. He was getting another damned tension headache, that particular malady having become an all too frequent occurrence over the past couple of months. But then Tricia was a headache…in spades! His voice edged with annoyance, he muttered, "If you don't mind, I'd like to save this discussion for a less public place."

The wind played with the thick, raven strands of his hair for a moment, picking them up and redistributing them in random patterns across his high forehead. Tricia had to forcibly restrain herself from reaching out to him, her fingers itching to spear through those wayward tendrils and smooth them back into place.

Such an inconsequential, feminine urge increased her frustration, and she snapped, "Then you'd better wait until I get home tonight, because you wouldn't want your secretary listening in on our conversation."

A slow grin curved his mouth as he drawled, "My office has been soundproofed."

That information effectively increased her tension, and she felt a thrill ripple through her body with the abruptness of summer lightning. Crossing her arms over her chest in an instinctively defensive manner, she rubbed her palms over the gooseflesh rising above her elbows and tried to offer up a smile for his benefit.

It was a weak effort at best, as was her attempt to inject a humorous note into their conversation. "You mean nobody will hear my tormented cries for help when you start to strangle me?"

"You may cry out," he murmured with gentle mockery, "but I assure you it won't be because my hands are around your neck. There are other areas on a woman's body that are far more sensitive to... torture."

She nearly choked at the husky sensual note that laced his voice with innuendo, but was far more disturbed by the jealousy she felt when she stared up at him. There was a gleam in his eyes that denoted a degree of macho confidence she deplored, especially when she considered just how he must have gained his experience of a woman's body.

Violently hating the thought of him with some faceless, oversexed female of doubtful virtue, she could imagine how much worse it would be if she'd spotted him in a restaurant having lunch with another woman. As she was learning first-hand, jealousy was not a calm, temperate emotion, and it had no basis in logic. Considering the conclusions she'd drawn, she wondered what had kept Marc from punching Donovan in the nose.

If he had it would have been all her fault, she acknowledged guiltily. When she'd asked Donovan to escort her to the dinner party last night, she had wanted to do more than make Marc aware of her independence. She had wanted to gain his attention, yes... but she'd also wanted to make him see her as a woman who was attractive to other men. In short, she'd wanted to make him jealous. She had used a friend to manipulate her husband, and realization of just how selfish she'd been made her cringe with shame at her behavior.

Without considering the advisability of total honesty at this point in their relationship, she blurted, "I'd never cheat on you with another man, Marc. My meeting with Donovan this afternoon was strictly business. From a few hints he dropped last night, I suspect he needs me to donate some time to counsel one of his kids."

Although his features assumed a sober cast, there was also a hint of guilt in the look he gave her. "It wasn't you I was worried about."

"But you said...."

"I didn't mean those accusations I made last night," he interrupted tautly. "I was disappointed when you weren't at home, and I let my temper get the best of me."

"It reminded you of all the times your mother wasn't there for you, didn't it?" she whispered in sudden understanding.

He reached out and cupped her warm cheek in his hand, and studied her face with quiet thoughtfulness. "You're as different from her as night is from day."

Her eyes closed as she remembered the anguish his accusations had cost her. "Oh, Marc, thank you for saying that. How I wish last night had never happened!"

"Perhaps it's better that it did," he remarked bluntly. "At least now I know I'm as capable of jealousy as the next man."

At this she brightened, her face flushing prettily. "You are?"

"Mm," he murmured. "Such primitive emotions are quite alien to me, my—"

He paused deliberately, and a rare smile lightened his features as he finished his sentence. "—Tricia."

The sound of her nickname on his lips completely shattered what remained of her defenses, and she never even noticed when several cars passed by them in quick succession. Nor was she aware of her feet moving as he guided her between the white painted lines of the crosswalk. She moved with automatic mindlessness, her thoughts concentrated solely on regulating her breathing.

Her lack of attention caused her to trip over the curb, and her flush deepened with embarrassment. "Excuse me, I..."

"So flustered," he murmured, his eyes glinting with humor as he took note of her heightened color. "Why, I wonder? It's not like we haven't had...conversations before."

DOUBLE YOUR ACTION PLAY...

"ROLL A DOUBLE!"

Peel off label & place inside

**CLAIM UP TO 4 BOOKS
PLUS A LOVELY
"KEY TO YOUR HEART"
PENDANT NECKLACE**

ABSOLUTELY FREE!

SEE INSIDE..

NO RISK, NO OBLIGATION TO BUY...NOW OR EVER!

GUARANTEED

PLAY "ROLL A DOUBLE" AND GET AS MANY AS FIVE GIFTS!

HERE'S HOW TO PLAY:

1. Peel off label from front cover. Place it in space provided at right. With a coin, carefully scratch off the silver dice. This makes you eligible to receive two or more free books, and possibly another gift, depending on what is revealed beneath the scratch-off area.

2. You'll receive brand-new Silhouette Desire® novels. When you return this card, we'll rush you the books and gift you qualify for ABSOLUTELY FREE!

3. Then, if we don't hear from you, every month, we'll send you 6 additional novels to read and enjoy. You can return them and owe nothing, but if you decide to keep them, you'll pay only $2.49 per book—a saving of 40¢ each off the cover price.

4. When you subscribe to the Silhouette Reader Service™, you'll also get our newsletter, as well as additional free gifts from time to time.

5. You must be completely satisfied. You may cancel at any time simply by sending us a note or a shipping statement marked "cancel" or by returning any shipment to us at our expense.

The Austrian crystal sparkles like a diamond! And it's carefully set in a romantic "Key to Your Heart" pendant on a generous 18″ chain. The entire necklace is yours free as added thanks for giving our Reader Service a try!

"ROLL A DOUBLE!"

PLACE LABEL HERE

SCRATCH HERE

?

SEE CLAIM CHART BELOW

225 CIS AELR
(U-SIL-D-05/92)

YES! I have placed my label from the front cover into the space provided above and scratched off the silver dice. Please rush me the free books and gift that I am entitled to. I understand that I am under no obligation to purchase any books, as explained on the opposite page.

NAME _____

ADDRESS _____ APT. _____

CITY _____ STATE _____ ZIP CODE _____

CLAIM CHART

⚅ ⚅	**4 FREE BOOKS PLUS FREE "KEY TO YOUR HEART" NECKLACE**
⚅ ⚄	**3 FREE BOOKS**
⚅ ⚃	**2 FREE BOOKS**

CLAIM NO.37-829

SILHOUETTE "NO RISK" GUARANTEE

- You're not required to buy a single book—ever!
- You must be completely satisfied or you may cancel at any time simply by sending us a note or shipping statement marked "cancel" or by returning any shipment to us at our cost. Either way, you will receive no more books; you'll have no obligation to buy.
- The free books and gift you claimed on this "Roll A Double" offer remain yours to keep no matter what you decide.

The double entendre was difficult to miss, and Tricia lowered her head as her lips pushed forward in a pout. "Stop teasing me."

He laughed knowingly, and returned his arm to its former position around her slim waist. "You have my complete attention, Tricia. Isn't that what all the game playing has been about these past few months?"

Her eyes widened briefly, but she quickly averted her attention from the intensity of his gaze. "I don't know what you mean."

They had nearly reached the large double doors leading into his office building, but before she could guess his intentions Marc gripped her shoulders and turned her to face him. "You've been doing your damnedest to irritate me lately, and now you're trying to make me jealous. I'm not a fool, so don't bother to deny it."

Refusing to be intimidated, she threw back her head and glanced up at him with a provoking smile. "And why would I do that?"

He hesitated a moment, and to her amazement his eyes held a regret that was echoed in his voice. "Because I've been a self-centered swine, and you're quite justifiably sick of being neglected."

Tricia's mouth opened and closed, but no sound emerged. She hadn't expected an apology from him, and she wasn't quite certain how to respond. Could Marc be as dissatisfied with their relationship as she was? she wondered breathlessly. Was he trying to tell her that he, too, wanted a new beginning?

As the tumultuous thoughts skittered around in her brain, Marc used the opportunity to urge her through the automated doors in front of them with visible impatience. She heard the muted swish as they opened and closed, but the elegance of her surroundings was lost on her. She took note of the dark mahogany panels inlaid against mellow cream walls in the central lobby with vague interest, her mind too full of exciting possibilities to bother with incidentals.

Seven

Tricia's feet sank into a thick, rust and cream carpet as they walked toward a pair of elevators located at the front of a long hallway. They passed several desks occupied by some of Marc's staff, and she responded to their polite greetings with a warm smile and a shyly uttered, "Good afternoon."

But Marc remained silent, acknowledging their presence with little more than a distant nod of his head. She studied the tense angle of his jaw with surprise, and a frown pleated her forehead when she noticed the firm, uncompromising set of his lips. There was a stillness in him that made her heart suddenly ache. He was a man set apart, she thought sadly, one who had forgotten, or never learned, how to respond to friendly overtures.

That supposition was more than proved by the surreptitious glances being sent their way by several of his employees. Even though they were exhibiting an impressive degree of deference toward their employer, there was no real emotion in the welcome Marc received. In short, she realized that her husband might command respect from those around him, but little else.

His distant attitude actively discouraged anything approaching the lighthearted camaraderie she shared with Eddy, and the knowledge saddened her. But soon the train of her thoughts shifted even further, and with shocked comprehension she realized that, with the possible exception of Edward and Martha Culcahy, there wasn't one person in her husband's life whom he could truly call a friend.

As though to reinforce the conclusion she'd reached, when Marc turned in her direction the expression of bored indifference on his face caused her to draw in a sharp breath. She was chilled to the bone by the reappearance of the cold, indomitable stranger she'd come to know so well during the year and a half they had been married. He was simply too mired in his own isolation, she decided pensively, and too invulnerable to outside influences to allow himself to be touched by anyone on more than a surface level.

The thought depressed her, and as if by some forbidding, dark alchemy, any burgeoning hope she had for their future together trickled away into nothing. In growing frustration she wondered how anyone, especially someone as woefully uncertain of her feminine allure as she was, could ever break through this man's iron-clad defences.

Her life had been ridiculously sheltered, she acknowledged with painful honesty, first by her parents, then under the strict guardianship of her brother Drew, and last but not least by the somewhat lackadaisical but still diligent Donovan. She'd had too many watchful eyes on her to be able to kick up her heels and fly free, which hadn't done much to garner her any real experience with the opposite sex.

And Marc was the kind of man who attracted scores of beautiful, chic women who could match his urbane sophistication in a way she could never hope to do. Although she'd made him aware of her dissatisfaction with their marriage, and he was apparently even willing to shoulder a portion of the blame, it wasn't enough. Simply admitting that there was a problem wasn't going to solve it.

Something of what she was thinking must have shown on her face, because as they entered the elevator Marc barely waited for the door to close before scowling at her. "I know I should have introduced you to my staff, but I'm hardly in the mood for polite introductions."

"Why should you be?" she countered in frigid tones. "There was nobody in the lobby you particularly wanted to make an impression on."

His big body tensed angrily. "What in hell is that supposed to mean?"

"You married me to impress the worthy with your wife's illustrious social background." She laughed dryly and gave a dismissive shrug of her shoulders. "Apparently your staff don't qualify as worthy in your eyes."

The door slid open at the fourth floor, saving her from the scathing denunciation she suspected hovered on her husband's lips. As she glanced over at him she noticed a muscle pulsing in his cheek, and when Marc gritted his teeth it was a sure indication of his displeasure with her. So... alluding to his cynical, condescending reasons for marrying her bothered him, did it? she thought with a tiny surge of triumph. Good! At least he wasn't treating her with the indifference he did everyone else around him.

A tiny smile of satisfaction curved her lips, which died the instant she noticed an elegantly garbed brunette exit a nearby office and walk toward them. Even in the rather austere cut of a gray suit and a severely plain white silk blouse, there was an earthy lushness to her approaching figure that made Tricia feel like a dowdy bean pole in comparison.

Her confidence was further shaken when a pair of vivid green eyes surveyed Marc's swarthy features with a predatory attention to detail. That avaricious look spoke volumes, and Tricia's protective instincts went on full alert. When the tip of the woman's small pink tongue darted out to moisten smiling, gloss-slickened lips, Tricia's alert system shifted over to "fire when ready."

How dare this...this thin-lipped female come on to Marc, especially in front of his wife? Reminding herself that the brunette had no way of knowing that she was his wife made no difference, and her fury escalated with a rapidity that made her breathless. After all, it was common knowledge that he was a married man, and there was such a thing as decent behavior, she thought indignantly.

But when she noticed the calculated, seductive sway of the other woman's snug-skirted hips as she glided across the hall, Tricia realized that a little inconvenience like a wife wouldn't stop this particular female if she wanted a man. And she wanted Marc! Tricia concluded hollowly, the certainty causing her to dig her fingernails into the soft leather of her shoulder bag.

"Marc, I'm glad I caught you."

Those vividly glowing, sultry eyes briefly surveyed Tricia and dismissed her presence with insulting rapidity, but her fatuously grinning husband certainly didn't seem to notice. "Have I forgotten an appointment, Alita?" he asked.

Placing a slender, scarlet-tipped hand against his muscular forearm, she laughed huskily. "Of course you haven't, but I finished going over the Bahamian contracts sooner than I expected, and there are a couple of potential problem areas I wanted to go over with you."

Tricia wondered sourly if Marc had an ulterior motive for staring so hard at the folder clutched to the other woman's chest, and her voice was as brittle as broken glass when she asked, "Aren't you going to introduce me, darling?"

The implied criticism brought Marc's head around in a rush, and there was a distinct warning in his narrow-lidded eyes as he gazed at her. He hesitated for long, tension fraught moments, but eventually complied with her wishes. "Tricia, this is the newest contract lawyer to join our staff, Alita Murray," he said.

Shifting his attention to the other woman, he stated abruptly, "Alita, my wife Patricia."

Tricia managed to stretch her mouth into a polite grimace, but it would never have passed inspection as a smile. "How do you do, Ms. Murray...or is it Mrs.?"

"I'm not married, Mrs. Everett."

She briefly shook the hand Tricia extended to her, having to release her hold on Marc to do so. "I tried it once, but found myself stifled by my husband's ridiculous demands on my time."

"Yes, a husband can be very...demanding."

As she spoke Tricia deliberately leaned against Marc's side, her voice husky as she glanced up at him from beneath her lashes. "Marc and I were just on our way to his office to discuss that particular subject, weren't we?"

"We certainly were." Although his words were bland, the arm he draped over her shoulders was more forceful than affectionate, and the press of his fingers as he gripped her flesh matched the severity of his gaze. Her mind immediately went blank, and she was almost relieved when Alita Murray broke the tense silence that had fallen between them.

"In that case, I won't interrupt you."

Tricia breathed a silent sigh of relief, but her moment of triumph didn't last long. Mark drew his gaze slowly away from hers, his manner immediately brisk and businesslike as he held out his hand for the contracts. "I'll take a look at them now."

For an instant Alita Murray glanced at Tricia, a malicious gleam in her cool green eyes. "I'm so sorry for interrupting your afternoon with Marc, Mrs. Everett."

I just bet you are, Tricia thought, but all she said was "No apology is necessary."

To her consternation, her stilted response had the opposite effect from the one she intended. Marc had released his hold on Tricia to peruse the contents of the folder, and as he heard Alita's sweetly spoken apology he lifted his head and smiled at the other woman. "As you see, Alita, my wife is very understanding."

Tricia's spine stiffened as she stared at her obtuse spouse with murder in her heart. Oh, is she? she thought furiously. Is she, indeed?

"I'm sure she is."

Then once more ignoring Tricia as though she didn't exist, Alita said, "By the way, I asked your secretary to remind you about the dinner party at Hillview next

Saturday night, Marc. You will be attending, won't you?''

When he hesitated, she protested his reluctance. "It is being given largely for your benefit, you know."

With a shrug he said, "My wife and I will be there."

His attention once more distracted by the papers he held in his hands, he moved to lean against the far wall. Thus it was Tricia who was forced by good manners to keep the conversation going. "Hillview?" she asked.

With Marc safely out of hearing range, Alita responded with a distinct note of mockery in her voice. "My uncle's Piedmont estate. He'll be pleased to meet you at last."

"Your uncle?" Tricia exclaimed faintly.

Looking like the cat that had just shoved its fangs into a bowl of cream, Alita said, "He's a merchant banker and an extremely influential man in business circles, Mrs. Everett. I'm trying to interest him in investing in Marc's newest project. If he does, several of his friends will automatically follow his lead. Uncle Peter's involvement in the Bahamian resort development will guarantee its success, with little or no risk to Marc's corporation."

Alita Murray was subtly but surely letting her know that she could provide Marc with more than his insipid, timid little wife ever could. There was an implied threat in the other woman's dulcet tones, and Tricia's heart sank to the level of her shoes. She was left in no doubt that this beautiful, self-assured female could match Marc on every level of his life, and that she also possessed a sophistication and intelligence that would be used ruthlessly if necessary. Alita was a vivid example of the kind of woman Tricia had always been intimidated by, one with a background and education similar to her own, whose career guaranteed a common ground between her and Tricia's husband.

Tricia's mind was spinning with conjecture, this newest threat to her marriage dismayingly obvious. "I'm surprised your uncle allows you to influence his business decisions."

"I'm his sole heir, and we're very fond of each other," Alita replied with a self-satisfied smirk. "Since he spent all of last week in the Bahamas with Marc and me, I'd say he respects my judgment."

Tricia fought to keep her expression serene, Alita Murray's words slicing through her like a knife. The thought of this woman and her husband spending time together in a romantic setting like the Bahamas was anathema to her, especially when she remembered all the lonely hours she'd spent waiting for him to come home.

Unwillingly she found herself wondering if a business relationship was all Marc intended sharing with the newest member of his staff, and her voice held a bitter inflection as she muttered, "How nice for you."

Marc had just returned to her side as she spoke, and a puzzled frown pleated his forehead as he took note of the tension emanating from his wife. "What's wrong?"

Your reasons for proposing to me were wrong, our marriage is wrong, and this black-haired piranha is wrong if she thinks she's going to sink her teeth into you! she thought with increasing indignation. But all she said was "Not a thing, Marc."

Her gaze locked with that of Alita Murray's in a silent declaration of war, and she smiled with a confidence she certainly didn't feel. "Ms. Murray and I were just getting to... know each other."

Still oblivious to any undercurrents, her husband tapped his forefinger against the folder in his hand and grimaced. "I'm going to have to call my New York office right away, so they can work up some necessary revisions over the weekend. We promised to fax these contracts to the Bahamas by Monday, and any delay can be crucial at this stage in our negotiations."

Tricia wanted to throttle him for his obtuseness, but merely said, "That's all right, darling. I was going to have to leave soon anyway. I have a three o'clock appointment, remember?"

"How wise of you to be so accommodating, Mrs. Everett."

Tricia didn't need Alita's approval, especially when it was uttered with such gloating sarcasm. Looking the other woman straight in the eye, she uttered her parting shot with poise and dignity. "It would be a mistake to underestimate me, Ms. Murray."

The angry flush that mottled the brunette's cheeks vastly restored Tricia's self-confidence, and she turned to Marc with a meaningful smile. "If you return my keys I'll be running along. I'll see you at home."

Extracting the keys from his inside coat pocket, he paused a moment to stare down at her lovely, curving mouth. When her lips parted on an indrawn breath his eyes darkened in response, and he swallowed heavily. Clearing his throat, he murmured, "I won't be late."

"I hope not." Leaning forward, she pressed a kiss into the cleft of his chin, and whispered, "You're not the only one who's impatient, darling."

His chest rose and fell quickly, and as she turned to leave he halted her departure by cradling her cheek in his hand. Oblivious to the other woman's presence, he pressed a heated kiss against Tricia's parted mouth. Her eyes widened in surprise, and then closed as she savored the pleasure of his embrace. When his head rose with satisfying reluctance, her lashes lifted and she gazed up at him in lingering bemusement. "What was that for?" she questioned huskily.

He grinned, and dropped a final kiss on the tip of her nose. "Just a little something on account."

Tricia was elated by Marc's open show of affection, and her feet barely touched the floor as she turned to leave. But when she caught sight of the expression on Alita Murray's face, her footsteps faltered betrayingly. Resentful green eyes speared into her like twin lasers, their depths filled with jealous hatred

and determined resolve. Tricia instantly realized that
she had made a dangerous enemy, and the knowledge
caused her stomach to clench sickeningly as the elevator doors closed behind her.

Eight

By the time he pulled into the driveway that evening, Mark wondered how a single day could be so long. The niggling headache he'd had earlier had metamorphosed into a real zinger, largely due to the female of the species. "Women!" his mind intoned forcefully. "They wreak havoc with a man's nerves." At the thought he closed his eyes against the shaft of sunlight that speared through the windshield of his car, and rested his aching head against the head rest attached to his bucket seat.

He had parked his BMW in the driveway beside his wife's sporty Corvette, and wondered why she hadn't taken the time to pull her car into the garage as was her usual habit. If she was planning to go over to Donovan Lancaster's place while he was at his city council meeting tonight, she could think again. If she needed to discuss counseling with one of Donovan's kids, she could do so during business hours. As things stood Marc was already as irritated as hell with her, and he didn't need another argument to set the seal on his foul mood.

Alita Murray had already made great strides in adding to the initial stress headache his wife had given him, he thought grimly, and if he was faced with one more example of feminine hysterics he was going to go right over the edge. Twisting the keys out of the ignition with more force than was strictly necessary, he returned to a slumped position against the bucket seat and stared blindly through the windshield at the triple doors of his garage.

Somehow poor Alita seemed to have gained the impression that Tricia had taken a dislike to her, and had actually wept at the possibility that she might have caused trouble between him and his wife. "I shouldn't have mentioned us being together in the Bahamas, Marc," she'd murmured brokenly, her moisture-glazed eyes wide with remorse as she gazed at him across his desk. "It gave her the wrong impression of our relationship, I know it did!"

"My wife wouldn't succumb to petty jealousy, Alita, especially without cause," he assured her.

She gave a laugh full of bitterness, and shook her head. "You don't understand women," she informed him with a suppressed sob. "I can't help my physical appearance, and the way I'm treated by members of my own sex is so unfair. Wives take one look at me, and before I know it I'm history. I love working for you, Marc. I feel you understand me as no one ever has before, and I can't tolerate the thought of that happening to us."

"It won't."

Although his voice had held gentle reassurance, he'd been fervently wishing she'd stop the waterworks. He hated it when women cried. Tears were one of the weapons his mother had used to make his father feel guilty for doubting her faithfulness, and this time he had only himself to blame for being subjected to them.

He'd been concentrating on those damned contracts this afternoon to the exclusion of everything else, and he hadn't even realized that his wife's behavior had been anything out of the ordinary. It hardly seemed in character for Tricia to be unkind to anyone, he thought perplexedly, especially someone she'd just met. Could Alita be right? he wondered. Surely Tricia wasn't suspicious of his relationship with his employee. If he was going to engage in an affair, he thought indignantly, he certainly wouldn't be stupid enough to do so with a member of his own staff.

Although the thought was reassuring, he winced when he remembered how that very possibility had once occurred to him. But he immediately pushed aside any guilt he felt, telling himself that what mattered was that he hadn't acted on the temptation the other woman had briefly presented to him in the Ba-

hamas. Hell, a man couldn't be convicted for having
an active imagination, he thought in an attempt to reaffirm his sense of grievance.

Alita was a beautiful, sensual female and he was a
man with normal urges. Of course he had fantasized
a bit. Any healthy male would have to be dead from
the neck down not to react mentally to a sexy woman—any sexy woman—in a like manner. But he'd
never seriously contemplated cheating on his wife.

That kind of disloyal behavior disgusted him.
Hadn't he learned about unfaithfulness and the kind
of misery it could cause at his own mother's knee? His
father had suffered the torments of the damned, his
trust shattered over and over again while his mother
made a mockery of their marriage. Marc would never
inflict that kind of suffering on his wife…never! And
yet according to Alita, Tricia was suspicious of their
association and had behaved toward her with undue
haughtiness and sarcasm.

Tiredly he pinched the bridge of his nose between
his thumb and forefinger, momentarily alleviating
some of the pressure building between his eyes. If what
Alita suspected was fact, how dare his wife believe him
capable of breaking his vows without a shred of evidence to back up her nasty-minded suppositions?

It was true that Alita Murray was a lovely woman,
but he hadn't hired her because of her looks. His reasons for adding her to his staff had been based entirely on logic and common sense, he thought with
self-righteous indignation. He had needed someone

conversant with contract law, and she had come to him with excellent qualifications.

"And did you believe Patricia unequivocally when she assured you that her meeting with Donovan Lancaster this afternoon was strictly business?" a troublesome voice straight out of his conscience probed. "You might not think she intends cheating on you, but you're still damned wary of her friendship with that bleeding heart liberalist. Why should Tricia's illogical dislike of Alita be any different? Aren't Lancaster's motives suspect in your mind, if for no other reason than that he's rich, good looking, and has a reputation with women?

"And he shares Patricia's advantaged upbringing," that mischievously verbose imp in his head reminded him, which was something to which the son of a coal miner could never aspire.

Marc acknowledged the truth of that thought with a cynical twist of his lips. He knew himself for what he was, a diamond in the rough, a self-made man with a sketchy education and a far from illustrious family background. Unlike his wife and her old family friend, he couldn't trace his antecedents past his grandparents. Even if he could, he decided with a bark of wry laughter, he doubted seriously that he would like what he found. With his luck, there had probably been more than one outlaw in the bunch.

Grabbing his briefcase, he hauled himself out of the car and slammed the door shut. He skirted the circular walkway that led to his front door, and cut straight across his well manicured lawn. The thing was as neat and uniform as a smooth green carpet, and Cully would have a fit if he caught him trampling so much as a single blade of grass. When he remembered the ramshackle house next door to his parents' that Cully had once lived in, a grin eased the tenseness of his mouth.

The weed-strewn yard had been filled with all the bits and pieces of mechanical junk Cully had felt necessary to survival, and he and Marc had spent many pleasant hours with their heads stuck under the hood of one derelict vehicle or the other. It was one of the few good memories he had of his childhood, yet he couldn't help thinking how the mighty had fallen. Now the old man was as house proud as a broody hen guarding a nest of eggs, but it would be more than Marc's life was worth to accuse him of such a thing.

By the time he entered the house, he was in a slightly better humor. He was certain that Alita had blown her meeting with Tricia completely out of proportion, and he wasn't even going to bother mentioning the other woman's insecure ramblings to his wife. That's all they were, he decided, just the uncertainty of a female who was essentially a man's woman. If his employee felt threatened by members of her own sex that was her problem, not his or Tricia's.

His feet echoed hollowly against the tile of the entry hall as he wandered toward the library, his eyes automatically searching the room as he headed for the Regency desk situated beneath the large, multipaned window along the far wall. He plopped his black leather case down on the smooth surface of the desk-top, unconcerned with the glowing patina of aged wood as he searched the backyard for signs of his wife.

She wasn't working in the garden as she sometimes did in the early evening, and nor was she walking be-side the black-bottomed pool, which resembled a small, ornamental lake and yet was as functional as any other swimming pool. He released his breath in a derisive sniff when he considered his boyish whimsy, which had played hell with the tempers of the com-pany he'd hired to build the thing. But he'd paid well for the privilege of turning his five acre estate into the kind of place he'd always dreamed of owning, and as with anything else it was money that did the talking.

An electrified fence circled his property, which in-cluded two other large, cottage-style homes that were out of sight of the main house behind a tall stand of juniper. These were lived in by the Culcahy's and their youngest daughter and son-in-law, and although he'd had his doubts when he had built the second house, the extended family situation seemed to be working out just fine. Cully sometimes groused a bit, but then Cully habitually grumbled about one thing or an-other.

Martha's other two children were quite a bit older than her last little fledgling, and both had married and moved out of state quite a few years ago. As a result Martha was inordinately attached to her youngest, whose husband Ben was employed as a teacher at an

elementary school in nearby Dublin. Marc also paid
Ben and a local man to help with some of the heavier
work around the place, a decision that had riled Cully
considerably when it had first been suggested. But for
the old man's sake he'd had to ignore his stiff-necked
pride, and had thought long and hard to find less
strenuous tasks to keep him feeling useful.

Removing the jacket to his suit, he flung it over one
shoulder and retraced his path to the stairs. When he
reached the upper landing, he turned in the direction
of the master suite and yawned tiredly. God! He
wished he didn't have to go out tonight, but the city
council meeting had been called to vote on the rezon-
ing of two areas in Hayward where he owned non-
commercial property, and he was anxious to hear the
council's final decision.

Alita Murray's uncle was a city councilman, and
he'd offered to sway as many members as he could in
Marc's favor. But Marc hadn't taken him up on his
offer, edgily reluctant to trust the man. His brow
wrinkled into a thoughtful frown as he entered the
comfort of the mauve and gold sitting room that bi-
sected his bedroom and his wife's. Dropping his jacket
on the back of a circular sofa, which was placed directly in front of a wall comprised entirely of glass, he
let his mind contemplate the advisability of doing any
kind of business with Peter Greer.

Marc hadn't realized that Alita was related to Greer
when he'd hired her, and now he wondered if he would
have done so had he known. The tycoon referred to

himself as a merchant banker, but only because he'd bought the damn bank. In reality the old shark had very sharp and deadly teeth that could rip an enemy to shreds if he didn't get what he felt was his due. And the man's influence, if some of the gossip he'd heard was true, wasn't always the result of associating with the upper echelon of polite society.

Marc didn't like the idea of judging a man on hearsay, but he was also hesitant about risking his own reputation. He'd worked long and hard to earn approval and prestige in the business community, and he wasn't about to jeopardize the firm he'd built by letting any hint of scandal attach to his name. Nor was he willing to relinquish control, which he had stated unequivocally to Alita.

But she had assured him that control of the Bahamian project would remain firmly in his own hands.

He also hadn't let her flattery of his business acumen, or his list of accomplishments go to his head. Instead he had leaned his elbows on his desk and formed a steeple with his fingers, glancing at her thoughtfully over the top of his hands. "Now why don't you tell me the real reason you want me to accept your uncle as an investor, Alita?"

Although her shoulders slumped betrayingly, her gaze was steadfast as she said, "Uncle Peter is a wonderful man, Marc. He took me in when my parents died, and paid for my upbringing and my education. I owe him more than I can ever repay, and I'd give anything to get him out of the depression he's fallen into because of that Decamo debacle. All of the gossip that resulted from the investigation has hurt his pride terribly, and he's looking for a way to regain his credibility. Your corporation has a sterling reputation, and an association with you could help him regain the respect he deserves.''

"It would also bring him in a hell of a big return on his initial investment,'' he responded dryly.

"There's always a measure of risk involved in a project of this size,'' she protested. "You know that as well as I do.''

Which was why he wasn't going it alone this time, he had acknowledged silently, and that admission was probably the reason he finally agreed to invite Greer to meet with him in the Bahamas. That and the plaintiveness of Alita's voice as she whispered, "Please . . . all I'm asking is that you talk to Uncle Peter, Marc. It would mean so much to me, and if you decide not to do business with him, I'll understand.''

Remembering that promise now, he wondered if she would understand or if he'd soon be looking for a new contract lawyer. He'd hate to have that happen. The woman was good at her job, but he wasn't comfortable with the notion of borrowing money from a member of her family. He nearly had all the financial backing he needed anyway, and his company could absorb the slack if necessary.

Still, he'd agreed to consider Greer's proposal for the Bahamian project, and he would keep his word. One of his corporate investigators was compiling a report on the other man, and he'd shelve his final decision until he had more concrete information at his fingertips.

That resolution easing his mind, Marc wandered over to the built-in wet bar in the corner and fixed himself a Scotch and water. Because of his father's example he rarely indulged in alcohol, but he felt in need of something a little stronger than coffee this evening. The pounding at the base of his skull was driving him crazy, and he felt as though someone had driven an ax through the center of his forehead.

Where the hell did Martha keep the aspirin? He was ready to storm the kitchen to ask her, when he remembered that she would be gone for the next couple of days. Tricia would know where they were hidden, he decided, scowling when he remembered that he didn't know where his wife was, either.

The rotten day he'd just spent, his frustration over the Bahamian project, his worry over his relationship with Tricia, and last but not least his little talk with Alita, had all combined to get the best of him. Thoroughly disgruntled, he slammed his empty glass down on the bar, flinching as pain shot through his head, and went in search of his wife. Forgetting to indulge his usual courtesy of knocking, he pushed open the door to her bedroom and crossed the threshold.

His tension was abruptly eased when he spotted a golden mass of curls spread out over a white satin pillow. He approached the bed slowly, his gaze absorbing the pleasing picture she made as she lay sleeping.

Her features were smooth and serene, and one hand rested beneath a delicately flushed cheek. Her rosy lips were slightly parted, the breath issuing from between them in sighing puffs.

As he watched, her long lashes fluttered and then lifted, revealing the crystal purity of her gaze. "Hi," she murmured, her voice husky from sleep.

Her smile caused him to catch his breath, and he slowly lowered himself onto the edge of the bed. "Hello," he responded quietly.

Hiding a yawn behind her slender fingers, she asked, "What time is it?"

He glanced at his watch. "Nearly five-thirty."

When she uttered a dismayed gasp he smiled at the guilty expression on her face, before allowing his gaze to wander over her somnolent body. She was clad in a silky cream camisole top with matching panties, and he observed the slim length of her legs with interest. His mouth curving appreciatively, he asked, "Waiting for me?"

"I left the office right after my three o'clock appointment, to give myself time to bathe and change for dinner." She yawned again, and glanced up at him sheepishly. "The bed was too inviting to resist."

"Especially with you in it," he murmured huskily.

At this, all traces of sleepiness disappeared from her eyes, and the delicate color in her cheeks deepened with embarrassment. "When did you get home?"

Recognizing her evasion with amusement, he stretched and rubbed his hand against the back of his neck. "About fifteen minutes ago. Gosh, I'm beat!"

Tricia noticed the deep lines of tension scoring each corner of his mouth, and suggested a shower and a short nap before they ate. "I defrosted one of Martha's casseroles, and it won't take long to heat it up in the microwave. I know this city council meeting is important to you, but it isn't scheduled to start until eight o'clock, is it?"

He shrugged, and said, "Yes, but I'd like to get there a little early. It will give me a chance to discuss the zoning issue with a few of the councilmen. Who knows, I might be able to affect the vote if I can convince enough of them to keep the zoning residential."

Marc had been unaware of the pain that briefly colored his expression as he moved his shoulders, but Tricia noticed the betraying wince immediately. "What's wrong? Do you have a headache?"

He nodded and once again winced. "A killer."

"You've been having too many headaches recently," she murmured in concern. "You're too tense over this newest project of yours, Marc."

Rising up on one elbow, she placed a cool hand on his forehead. "You're not feverish."

Although his eyes closed in appreciation of her soothing touch, he muttered, "Don't fuss."

"So who's fussing?"

Shifting into a sitting position, she efficiently began to unknot his dark tie. Once that task was completed her fingers moved to the buttons on his pale blue dress shirt, not halting her task until his belt was unfastened and she'd pulled the material free of his slacks. As she worked, one of the dainty straps of her camisole fell from her shoulder, and he bent and placed his lips against the small indentation it had left on her creamy skin.

"Mm," he sighed contentedly, "don't stop now. You're just getting to the good part."

"You're terrible," she laughed, slapping at the hand that began to reach for her lace-covered breast. "You have a headache, remember?"

"Mmm, yes. But what I can't forget is what you said to me this afternoon."

Arching her neck to facilitate his roving lips, she stammered, "What...what particular remark a-are you referring to?"

His mouth deserted the sweetly indented hollow at her throat, and the eyes that met hers were slumberous with desire. "You told me that I wasn't the only one lacking in patience, remember?"

His forefinger began to trace the ridge of her collarbone, and a triumphant smile spread across his mouth when she shivered. Quite pleased with the result of his effort, he drawled, "Aren't you going to prove it to me now, sweetheart? In case you haven't noticed, I came home earlier than usual."

Tricia felt as though her throat was caught within the unyielding clamp of a giant vise, and she fought to draw in enough oxygen to allow speech. "That's because you're unwell."

His tongue found the whorls and indentations of a shell-like ear. "I'm feeling better by the minute."

As Marc voiced the words, he suddenly realized how true they were. The softness of his wife's flesh beneath his hungry mouth and the sweet scent of her flesh had acted on him like a magic elixir, and his headache had faded to a dull throb at the base of his neck. But the throb at another strategic location in his body was the one he was concerned with most at the moment, and his fingers began to toy playfully with the other dainty strap on her camisole.

Tricia watched that darkly tanned hand slide lower over her partially exposed breast, and felt a melting sensation in the pit of her stomach. She had always been ridiculously vulnerable to Marc's undoubted sensuality, which was part of the problem with their marriage. His experience intimidated her. She didn't feel like an equal partner in their relationship, and she was especially uncertain in the bedroom. What Marc could have taught her she had been at first too shy, and later too insecure, to learn, and he had been much too convinced of her ladylike sensibilities to persist in her education.

Ladylike sensibilities be damned, she thought defiantly, she was a woman! For a long time she'd suspected that she was frigid, and it had taken a rather embarrassingly in-depth conversation with her sister-in-law to convince her otherwise. Maria had suggested a couple of books that might help, and after that she had haunted the library and bookstores looking for everything pertaining to human sexuality she could find on the shelves. There had been an amazing selection to choose from, and her self-improvement course had proved enlightening to say the least.

Some of the material she'd perused had been clinical, both on a bio-physiological as well as a psychological level. But only now was she beginning to realize how resentful she'd become of that rigid control Marc exercised over his emotions, finally understanding how his restraint had left her at the mercy of her own emotions. As a result she had made every effort to hide her vulnerability from him, but to do so she'd had to assume a demeanor that had left her frozen inside and unable to fully respond to his lovemaking.

Now she had actually bolstered her courage enough to begin planning his seduction, and yet here she was allowing him to call the shots once again. Well ... it wasn't going to happen ... not this time! They would make love when she was ready, and that would be when she was strengthened by the knowledge of her own desirability. Never again would she merely be Marc's means of scratching an itch, she vowed silently, because from now on she intended to be the flea that bit him.

The thought caused mirth to bubble up in her throat, and before he could guess her intentions she rolled to the other side of the bed and jumped to her feet. "Come back here," he protested in a deep-throated growl.

"What you need is a massage," she remarked cheerfully, ignoring the dissenting shake of his head. "Why don't you take a quick shower while I gather together the magic ingredients?"

Marc rose and studied her overly animated features dubiously. "Have you ever given a massage?"

"No, but kneading a few sore muscles can't be all that difficult."

A slow smile curved his lips as he informed her softly, "Then I'll need a full body massage. Do you have any oil you can rub over my skin?"

Determined to hang on to her composure by any means possible, she plopped her hands on her hips and eyed him with wickedly dancing eyes. "Will vegetable oil work?"

His expression startled, he blurted, "No, it damn well won't! I'm not a pork roast."

No, he certainly wasn't, she mused breathlessly as a mental image of her hands caressing his glistening, oil-slicked flesh popped into her mind. Her mouth went dry as a bone and she quickly ducked her head, swallowing what little saliva that remained in her mouth with a great deal of difficulty. This brainstorm of hers was threatening to become a bit more complicated than she'd planned, she realized, sneaking another look at her husband.

What she saw made her squirm nervously, as she once again evaded those knowing eyes. Now she'd done it, she decided, wondering why she always managed to back herself into corners. Maria accused her of leaping first and looking later, and she was beginning to think her friend was right. And if the look on Marc's face was anything to go by, the sadistic beast was enjoying this situation to the fullest. He was probably expecting her to back away and bolt like a frightened rabbit, and at the thought she stiffened her spine. She'd show him she was made of sterner stuff than that!

Tilting her rounded chin in the air, she somehow managed to maintain an attitude of nonchalance, which was completely erroneous. "There's this skin softener I bought that will do the trick."

At his dubious expression, she added, "Don't worry, it's unscented."

His heavy brows rose in a teasing arc. "Flowers don't turn you on, hmm?"

"N-not particularly," she stammered, not liking the way this conversation was going.

"They turn me on," he continued musingly, his eyes taking on a slumberous quality. "That's the way you always smell, like a spring bouquet freshly plucked from a field of clover."

"That's my perfume," she blurted stupidly.

His glance slipped downward, and he pointedly moistened his lips with the tip of his tongue.

If she thought her former outburst the height of idiocy, in her opinion the explanation that followed sounded even more ridiculous. "It's Maria's favorite scent, and after I tried some of hers I was hooked. I—I buy it at a perfumery in the mall, but it isn't always in stock. I usually find it in the store d-during Christmas, and..."

Her stammering voice dwindled into a silence so loud she thought her eardrums would burst. Closing her eyes as she muffled a groan, she whirled on her heel and headed for the bathroom that adjoined her bedroom. She didn't dare glance over her shoulder when she heard Marc laughing behind her, and nor did she contemplate pausing to ask him what was so darn funny. She already knew the answer, and it wasn't one that raised her self-confidence to any appreciable levels.

Decorated in pastel tones of lavender, pale rose, and cream, her bathroom failed to have its usual calming effect. The rose basin, toilet, and step-down oval tub were mere obstacles to be circumvented, and the wallpaper with its tiny lavender and pink flowers on a cream-colored background suddenly irritated her eyes. Even though she was barefooted as she stomped around the room, she didn't have the presence of mind to appreciate the plush rose carpet that saved her from injury.

Instead she kept muttering beneath her breath as she collected the materials she needed, until a wave of determination simultaneously steadied her temper and her trembling hands. "So... he wants a full body massage, does he?" she mused with a mischievous grin. "Boy, is he ever going to get one!"

Glancing at her reflection in the single mirrored wall, she noted the light of battle in her eyes with satisfaction. Though she hadn't planned ahead as carefully as she'd intended, she suddenly knew the time was right for Marc's seduction. He might not be a pork roast, but he was definitely a cooked goose.

Eagerly she placed the lotion and towels she'd collected on the cream-and-mauve-shaded counter, and reached into a drawer for her shower cap. Tucking the clean strands she'd washed that morning inside the plastic covering, she then moved toward the glass-enclosed shower in the corner.

What woman worth her salt needed a sexy dress to drive her husband crazy? she thought, beginning to strip off her camisole without a smidgen of concern for the delicate fabric. Her panties went the way of the top, and she stepped on them both as she reached for the stainless steel faucets. Adjusting the spray to a fine mist, she stepped inside and heard the door close with a firm, oddly reassuring click.

Nine

Marc jerked to a surprised halt as he reentered his wife's bedroom, his breath catching as he surveyed the scene before him. The brass-trimmed chandelier overhead was dimmed to its lowest setting, effectively shadowing the room's furnishings. The gas logs in the fireplace were surrounded with crackling fingers of flame, while Tricia knelt in front of the blaze with her hands folded in front of her, her expression serene.

She could be the resurrection of Eve, he decided, the epitome of perfection in any man's eyes. Her hair hung in a golden fall to her shoulders, which were bare of any adornment save the shimmering glow of her skin. Her eyes gleamed with the luster of aquamarines, their depth and purity highlighted by the dusky flush coloring her cheeks. Her lips wore only a blushing tint from nature's palette, their fullness moist and parted in a smile to reveal pearly white teeth.

As was the case with him, her only covering was a fluffy white towel. Unfortunately hers was larger than the one he'd hitched around his lean hips, and it covered her completely from the tops of her rounded breasts to just above her dimpled knees. The knot that held the separate edges of terry-cloth material together was located slightly off-center, and his pulse beat accelerated when he thought of how easy it would be to part those concealing folds. One good yank and....

"Are you ready?" her soft voice inquired.

He blinked and stared at her blankly, his mind still grappling with the vision of a fallen towel and luscious pink and white skin. Was he ready? he asked himself, unable to believe that she'd even bothered to ask such a ridiculous question. Taking a couple of steps forward, he paused uncertainly. "Uh, where do you want me?"

"Inside of me," his brain screamed. The answer his imagination had formed seemed to echo endlessly within his skull as he mentally urged her to reply in a like manner. But her only response was to gesture toward the extra towels spread out on the carpet. Until then he hadn't even noticed them, which said a great deal for the distracted state of his mind.

"Why don't you lay here in front of the fire," she suggested with a smile. "That way you won't get cold."

There wasn't any danger of that happening, but he followed her instructions to the letter. Stretching out on his stomach, he pillowed his forehead on his arms and closed his eyes. "Are you comfortable?" she asked after she waited a few seconds for him to stop squirming.

Considering the condition of his body below the waist, he decided it would be more politic to evade the question. Grunting an affirmative while he shifted his hips a little more to one side, he said, "Maybe you'd better start at my neck, Tricia. I'm...uh, pretty tense."

"Is that where most of your discomfort is?"

Damn! Every word she spoke seemed to keep his thoughts centered underneath his towel, which was beginning to chafe some very sensitive skin. His voice a little gruffer than usual, he muttered, "Hell's bells!"

Tricia couldn't understand him, and her breath wafted against his ear when she leaned forward. "What did you say?"

"I hear bells."

"Oh, your poor head," she murmured, gently running her hand over his hair. "Your ears must be ringing. Maybe you have a pinched nerve in your neck."

"Something's pinched, all right."

She began running both thumbs up and down the base of his skull, applying a firm but comfortable pressure to his spinal column. With a sigh of pleasure, he groaned, "That feels wonderful."

Encouraged by his praise, Tricia paused to warm some lotion between her palms and soon progressed to his broad shoulders. Repeatedly she pressed his spinal cord with her thumbs and then fanned out to the rounded edges of his upper arms, her fingers kneading as she again worked her way inward. Slowly she kept up the soothing massage until she reached the hollow at the base of his spine. She had also reached the edge of the towel.

"Do you mind if I take this off?" she asked, her voice quivering slightly. "It's in my way."

Marc couldn't see her smile, which widened delightedly when he moaned an unintelligible reply. Taking his response as permission to proceed, she carefully worked the towel free of his torso. His buttocks were whiter than the rest of him, and quite impressively firm as she began to squeeze the tense flesh with the aid of both hands and a dollop more lotion.

"Relax," she murmured. "The massage isn't going to work if you don't help me a little."

"Oh, it's working," he groaned. "Believe me, it's working just fine."

His chest began to rise and fall with the force of an out-of-control metronome, and it was everything Tricia could do not to chortle out loud. She had worked her way down to the top of a brawny thigh now, and as one of her hands moved between his legs she felt the shudder that wracked his body. This time her smile was one of smug satisfaction. "Is the pain easing up a little?"

"Getting worse," he gasped. Marc didn't know how much more of this he could take, but he was going to die trying to take it all. While another shiver shook him, he deliberately widened the space between his legs to further facilitate her wandering hands.

But when she whispered, "Poor baby," and he felt her mouth press against the base of his spine, it was enough to make him howl like a banshee. Rolling over abruptly, he pinned her with an indignant gaze. "You little devil, you're deliberately tormenting me."

With a teasing pout, she complacently eyed his arousal and widened her eyes in mock innocence. "Funny, it looks to me like you're enjoying yourself."

Marc crossed his arms behind his head, and grinned up at her. "Oh, I am," he remarked complacently. "Why don't you start on my front now, sweetheart. I have a few aches there that urgently need attention."

Tricia felt a sense of freedom she'd never experienced before. For the first time she was taking the initiative, and Marc seemed to actually be pleased by her boldness! Yet now that he was facing her, some of the debilitating shyness she'd always suffered from whenever they were intimate began to return, and she lowered her gaze to his chest.

Panicking briefly, she bit down on her lower lip. "Would y-you close y-your eyes?" she stammered.

To her amazement he did as she requested, his lashes lowering as a smile curved his mouth. "Is this better?"

She let her hands answer for her. With shy wonder she began to touch him, not even trying to pretend that these caresses were therapeutic. With feather softness she ran her fingers across his shoulders and upper arms, pausing to grip his bulging biceps with more force. Then she traced an inward path, and began to winnow through the dark hair on his chest with the tips of her fingers.

"Do you like touching me there?" he asked tightly.

"Yes."

Her reply was little more than a treble of sound, but it seemed to satisfy him. "Where else would you like to touch me?"

Her hands faltered at his question, but she answered honestly. "Everywhere."

His teeth clenched together, but he managed to bite out two succinct words. "Do it!"

She did, and Marc felt as though he was stretched out on a rack. His muscles tightened torturously, but there was no way he was going to call a halt. This was what he'd dreamed of, and he wasn't about to stop his woman when she was on a roll. How could he ever have thought her cold and unresponsive? he wondered, incredulous at his own blind stupidity. How in heaven's name could he have imagined her indifferent to him?

Then she cupped him gently between her hands, and every rational thought flew out of his head as he began to writhe at the pleasure she was giving him. "Oh, Tricia," he cried, jerking his forearms from behind his head so he could clutch at the towel spread out at his sides. "Oh, sweetheart ... yes!"

Marc's eyes flew open and he reached for her. In a single motion he tore off her covering and pulled her on top of him. While his hands probed every inch of her silky soft back and rounded buttocks, his mouth ate at hers with a voracious hunger. Her breath became his, her moans his, her ecstasy his. Their tongues duelled and fought each other for supremacy, but neither needed to win the battle. They were giving and taking in equal measure, and it was good ... so good!

Gripping her waist, he ended the kiss only to free his mouth for other delights. He bit at the pulsing chord in her neck with a force just short of painful, and his mind reeled when she cried aloud in pleasure. Then he lowered his head further, the hands that spanned her waist contracting as he enveloped a tight pink nipple with his lips.

He began to suckle strongly, and he savored the flavor of her sweet flesh as he forced her thighs to part and bend until she straddled him. To his amazement she not only complied with his unspoken demand, but she aided him by rising up on her knees until she was right where he wanted her. Completely out of control, he threw his head back and arched his hips. Lowering her onto his aching shaft, he suddenly thrust

into her melting heat with a force that shocked him
into a return of sanity.

"Damn . . . did I hurt you?" he cried.

Tricia merely closed her eyes and shook her head,
trembling with the sensations gripping her in seductive talons. Eagerly she reached out and braced her
hands against his chest, and then she began to move
on him with ever-increasing confidence. With a sigh,
she murmured, "It's . . . wonderful. I feel like I'm . . .
flying."

"Then take me with you," he groaned. "Take me
with you, sweetheart."

They took each other, soaring higher and higher as
they strove to reach that highest pinnacle of pleasure
together. Voices whispered and cried out, hands
touched and fondled, and mouths sought to drain each
drop of sweetness from moistening flesh. Then they
were there, and as Tricia began to convulse around
him, Marc followed her lead with a cry of completion
as triumphant as her own.

Long minutes passed as the pulsing spasms began to
ease into quiet ripples, and when he could finally move
again Marc tightened his arms around her. Tricia
curled on top of his big body with an exhausted murmur, and he held and caressed her into calmness again.
Then in deeply shaken tones, he said, "You just shattered every one of my preconceptions, sweetheart."

Surprise made her stiffen, and she lifted herself up
until she was able to study his solemn features. "Are
you . . . are you angry with me?"

As he acknowledged the reason for her uncertainty, Marc's eyes closed on a wave of self-disgust. "It's myself I'm angry with, for being so willfully blind."

Pulling her head down, he pressed his lips to hers. "This is the way you like it, isn't it? Wild and free and completely natural. But I always held back with you, because I never knew you wanted me like this. I never imagined all the sweet passion you were keeping from me."

Delicately she dipped her tongue into the cleft in his chin, smiling when his lips parted and he drew in a startled breath. Whispering the words into his mouth, she said, "I didn't know, either, not at first. And then I was too shy to tell you, and too afraid you'd think badly of me if I showed you."

Tenderly clasping her face between his hands, he kissed her with all the passionate tenderness she could have wished for. When the kiss ended he looked at her, remorse shadowing his beautiful dark eyes. "What a fool I've been," he remarked stiltedly. "You were like no woman I'd ever known before, Tricia. So gentle and sweet and innocent. I was terrified of hurting you, either physically or emotionally. So I kept my wilder urges under control, and in doing so I accomplished the very thing I was trying so hard to prevent. I made you afraid to respond to me, didn't I?"

"It doesn't matter anymore," she assured him.

Sighing with contentment, she snuggled her head into the indentation between his shoulder and collarbone, which seemed to have been fashioned expressly for her. Reluctantly she added, "I guess it's time you started dressing."

His lips slid over her forehead, down the side of her face, and ended up at her temple. "Why?"

"You'll have to be leaving for your meeting soon, and you need to have dinner first."

His tongue began to dip inside her ear as he again asked, "Why?"

Giggling and squirming simultaneously, she punched him in the chest. "Because you'll be late, and I don't want you fainting from hunger once you get there."

Suddenly he jackknifed into a sitting position, carrying her with him. His laughter joined hers as he rose to his feet with her still in his arms, and began walking toward the bed. "Where are we going?" she demanded with feigned haughtiness.

"Not to get dressed, that's for damn sure!"

To her chagrin her stomach chose that moment to growl, and he groaned as he dumped her on top of the bedspread. Shaking his head, he eyed her resignedly. "Don't you dare move from this spot," he warned. "I'll go downstairs and heat up some of that casserole you told me about, and then I'm going to have you for dessert."

"We'll have each other for dessert," she corrected, at last fully conversant with her womanly rights.

"Whatever," he murmured, barely pausing long enough to don a robe before striding from the room in a fever of impatience.

* * *

Tricia climbed out of the pool and slicked back the sopping wet hair from her forehead. Her eyelashes were beaded with moisture, and she blinked rapidly to clear her vision as she glanced around her brother's backyard. He and Maria had only moved into their new home a month ago, and this party was in the nature of an impromptu housewarming. The sneaky duo had deliberately delayed formal invitations, in order to avoid receiving housewarming gifts. It would have served them right if everybody had already made other plans for the day, but knowing Maria she would simply have invited them to show up the following Saturday. As Tricia had mentioned to Eddy, Maria hated formality almost as much as Tricia did!

She was reaching into her polka-dotted canvas beach bag when the subject of her thoughts whispered clandestinely from behind her. "What magic incantation did you perform on Marcus?"

Spinning around with a laugh, Tricia glanced toward a tree-shaded corner of the yard. There stood her husband in the midst of a male bonding ritual, gesturing with one hand as he said something to make the other men laugh. "I've never seen him this . . . this social," Maria concluded in awestruck tones.

To her annoyance a vivid blush darkened her already sunkissed face, and Maria's eyebrows shot up in amusement. "So all those books you've been studying over the past couple of months bore fruit, did they?"

Dragging the comb through her hair with unnecessary energy, Tricia found the grass tickling her bare toes fascinating as she mumbled, "Shouldn't you be busy slaving in the kitchen for this barbecue?"

"Everyone brought a dish to share," she retorted with a gesture at the women hovering around an already laden picnic table.

Feeling inordinately exposed by her friend's unabated interest, Tricia plopped her bag down on top of the lounge chair she had earlier appropriated. Grabbing for the gauze cover-up she had left draped over the back of the chair, she slipped it over her emerald green bikini with a disgruntled sniff. "Then go open a bag of potato chips or something."

"You were the one who brought the chips and dip and canned beverages," Maria reminded her as she grabbed her arm and began dragging her toward the kitchen of the lovely, split-level house built in a charming, mock Tudor design. "You can come and help me carry out the goodies and tear open the bags."

Although she willingly went to help Maria in the kitchen, which she'd intended to do anyway after her brief swim, Tricia managed to field her long-time friend's questions with the ease of practice. It wasn't as easy to ignore the smirks and knowing looks her sister-in-law sent in her direction, but she was still too filled with wonder over the night she'd just spent with her husband to want to share any confidences.

As she helped set the table and chatted with the other women around her, Tricia's mind spun with sensual images and remembered passion. Her eyes constantly sought Marc through the crowd cluttering the large, beautifully landscaped grounds, and when their eyes connected the look in his whisked the breath right out of her lungs. Her tasks completed, she finally managed to steal away to the relative privacy of the deserted lounge chairs set up on the opposite side of the yard from the food.

Stretched out on its colorfully woven surface, her thoughts drifted pleasantly as she soaked up the sunshine beating down on her from a cloudless blue sky. She heard the creak of the lounger beside her as someone invaded her snatched seclusion, but didn't bother to open her eyes. Shouts of laughter and the sound of energetic splashing came from a nearby swimming pool, while a chlorine scented breeze tickled her nostrils. A sensation of well-being permeated her somnolent body, and a tiny smile curved her mouth as she drifted away on a cloud of memory.

But the voice that emerged from the direction of the creaky lounge chair at her side sounded distinctly disgruntled. "I knew I shouldn't have let you answer that phone last night."

Lazily she angled her head until she was able to focus on her husband's scowling features. He had risen up on one elbow, and was surveying the brevity of her attire the way a hungry cat would stare at a delectably furry rodent. "You seem to be enjoying yourself."

The smile he gave her was more of a leer as he muttered, "I would have enjoyed spending the day in bed even more."

Her brows assumed a mocking slant. "Are you that tired, you poor old thing?"

"I'll show you tired," he said threateningly, leaping to his feet before she could do more than squeal. In a single motion he lifted her into his arms, his eyes sparkling wickedly as he began to carry her toward the pool.

Delighted with this unfamiliar, teasing and absolutely delightful side to her husband's personality, her hands wrapped around his neck in a loving hug. But when he paused at the edge of the pool her arms formed a stranglehold, as she glanced warily down at the water. Charlie and Lynette Holcomb, the two youngsters Maria had fostered until Charlie was old enough to assume responsibility for his sister, headed in their direction with yelps of glee. "Toss her this way, Mr. Everett," Charlie shouted. "I'll drown her for you."

Lynette splashed her brother in the face. "I'll protect you, Trish!"

By this time Maria had joined the fray, her black eyes dancing as she strolled in their direction. Obviously satisfied to have this opportunity to score off Tricia for failing to satisfy her curiosity, she said, "Enjoy yourself, but don't get any blood in my pool, Charlie."

Glaring at her accusingly, Tricia muttered, "You turncoat. So much for friendship!"

"I married your brother," Maria retorted smugly. "Now that I'm a member of the family you have to put up with me."

Tricia tilted her chin haughtily, while prudently tightening her grip on her grinning husband. With a disdainful snort, she warned, "I'll tell on you."

At the threat Maria cupped her hands around her mouth, and yelled across her backyard at a tall, sinfully handsome blond male. Drew Sinclair was wearing a grease-spattered butcher block apron over his bathing suit, as he turned hamburgers on a barbecue grill with more enthusiasm than skill. "Darling, is it all right if Charlie drowns your sister?"

"I've wanted to do it for years," he yelled back, waving in their direction with a spatula. "Be my guest."

Charlie started to thank him, but his mouth quickly filled with water when his sister snuck up behind him and leaped on his head. Marc and Maria laughed at the youngster's antics, but Tricia wasn't willing to let the opportunity to needle her brother pass. "See if I ever come to another one of your barbecues," she hollered indignantly.

Glancing back toward Maria, she uttered the ultimate threat. "If you aren't nice to me, I won't sit for you when the baby's born."

With a toss of her long black hair, Maria eyed her complacently and patted the small bulge in her tummy.

"I never thought of that," she admitted with a reluctant sigh. "If I let Charlie drown you, I'll be losing a potential patsy."

Grimacing at Marc, Maria said, "You'd better not throw her to the sharks, boss. A good sitter is hard to find, and she'll be the baby's aunt. I won't have to pay her for the privilege."

Maria's employer quirked a bold black eyebrow in her direction. "My wife insulted my manly pride."

At this the other woman gave Tricia a look of approval. "How did she do that?"

Marc told her, and she laughed up at him in response. "Why you poor old sensitive thing, you."

His eyes narrowed warningly. "Do you want that promotion I promised you after junior is born?"

"It's already been approved by your board of directors," she responded smugly. "Now that I'm a corporate executive, you have to have their vote before you can demote me. Anyway, you already gave Marge my job as apartment manager."

Feigning reluctance, he loosened his grip on Tricia's knees. But instead of placing her on her feet, he slowly slid her down his nearly naked body. She caught her breath as his chest hair cushioned her breasts and his hips aligned themselves with hers, and somehow was unable to tear her gaze away from the meltingly intense orbs devouring her face.

"Oops! I'd better go help the chef with those hamburgers," Maria murmured on a thread of laughter. "Join us when you finish, um, talking."

"Are you hungry?" Marc murmured in strangled accents.

Tricia's response was eager, if a bit breathless. "Oh, yes!"

Without another word Marc released her and grabbed her hand, pulling her toward the nearby gate in the Sinclairs' fence. He snatched his shirt and her cover-up as they passed, but her beach bag was left discarded on the lawn. "It's rude to sneak off in the middle of a housewarming party," she admonished without any real conviction in her voice.

"Then we won't sneak." Much to her consternation he turned his head and bellowed across the yard. "Have to leave now, Drew. Emergency. Your sister needs immediate attention. Enjoyed the party."

As they passed through the gate, ribald shouts and laughter followed their progress. "Oh, Lord," she moaned as she ran to keep up with her husband's hurried strides. "I'll never live this down!"

Holding open their car door, his black eyes glinted down at her with devilish intent. "Do you care?" he murmured softly.

Her heart in her eyes, she whispered, "Not a bit!"

Marc glanced at the cost prospective spread over his desk, and glanced at the woman seated across from him with grim disapproval. This was the second time this week Alita had called him at home, insisting that it was imperative he return to the office to advise her regarding the newest glitches in the Bahamian project. As he'd discovered the first time, his advice could have waited.

"What do you think, Marc? Should we allow Bergenstein to get away with increasing the cost percentages on the restaurant construction?"

"Since the timber industry took an unexpected dive last week, I don't see where Bergenstein had any other options. I also don't see why this couldn't wait until tomorrow's meeting to be discussed, Alita."

Alita lowered her head, hiding the anger that leaped to life in her eyes. In tones carefully calculated to convey regret, she said, "I was certain you wouldn't want to arrive at the meeting unprepared."

She was right, but she could have "prepared" him over the phone. He and Tricia had been in the middle of dinner when Alita's call had come through, and Martha had made no attempt to hide her disapproval when she'd handed him the portable phone. "Can't that woman let you enjoy a meal in peace?"

She had stomped off muttering beneath her breath, but Tricia had simply continued eating without uttering a sound. Even when she'd kissed him goodbye at the door, not a word of criticism had passed her lips. He'd found himself wondering if she even cared that their evening together had been disturbed, and that had made him more abrupt in his departure than he'd intended to be.

The truth was, he wasn't too certain what to think about the change in his relationship with Tricia. He seemed to be spending his days in a sensual haze, and his nights in a fever of passion. But their level of communication had not seemed to improve along with the physical rapport they'd achieved, and he was beginning to realize that sex, however good, might not be the only obstacle they needed to overcome in their marriage.

Damn! The woman had his mind spinning like a whirling dervish and his body perpetually aching. He felt completely out of control, and he didn't like the sensation one little bit. His thoughts of her were becoming obsessive, and even work wasn't able to provide the panacea it had in the past. Several times this past week he'd tried to talk seriously with Tricia about their relationship, but somehow or other they always ended up in bed.

Each time they made love was better than before, and his inability to resist her touch weakened his determination to establish a more open relationship. Although she gave herself to him with an eagerness that never failed to amaze and delight him, he sensed that she was still holding a part of herself away from him. He was beginning to hunger for something more, and being unable to put his finger on exactly what was missing from their marriage was frustrating the hell out of him.

And Alita Murray's unintentional interference wasn't helping him gain a closer understanding with his wife, he decided tiredly. With that thought in mind, his voice was harsh as he informed her, "From now on, I would prefer not to have my evenings disturbed."

Straightening abruptly, she apologized with stilted reluctance. "I'm sorry, but I thought this project took top priority in your life."

He studied the pinched disapproval evident in her tightly compressed lips, and felt a brief wave of pity for this woman who reminded him too much of himself before he'd married Tricia. Easing the aggravated note in his voice, he said quietly, "My wife does that."

Two hectic spots of color dotted her cheeks, and her hands clenched briefly before she rose to her feet. "Forgive me for being overzealous, but I only have your welfare at heart, Marc."

Rising to his feet, he nodded. "Be careful driving home."

Marc took a quick shower in the hallway bathroom so he wouldn't wake Tricia, and felt the familiar surge of adrenaline pumping in his bloodstream as he approached his bedroom. These past few days she'd been sharing his bed, and one of the subjects he wanted to discuss with her was making the arrangement permanent. For the first time in his life he felt less of a need for his own space, and more of a need for a warm, fragrant body to cuddle up to in the dark.

The realization put a wry smile of self-acknowledgment on his face, which disappeared the instant he noticed the empty bed in front of him. With a muffled curse he strode through the sitting room and entered Tricia's private sanctum. She was laying on her side with one hand cradling her sleep-flushed cheek, her other arm spread across the bed as though in search of something.

The brief spurt of anger he'd felt when he discovered her missing from his bed disappeared, and was replaced by a surge of tenderness so strong he felt the ache clear to his chest. He had been the one to insist on separate rooms, he recalled bitterly, and if she felt she needed an invitation to share his, he and he alone was the one to blame.

Slowly he turned, intending to return to his lonely isolation, when a husky, rather hesitant voice called his name. Bending over her, he brushed her forehead with his lips, and whispered, "Go back to sleep."

A lump the size of a boulder formed in his throat when two soft, loving arms circled his neck. "Stay with me."

With a husky murmur he stripped the towel from around his waist, and sought the warmth and comfort that was being so sweetly offered to him. As he cradled her in his arms and she relaxed back into sleep, he began to face a truth that shattered every one of the defences he'd built around his life. He felt himself breaking apart and reforming, and it was nearly dawn before he was able to accept what had happened to him. Somehow Tricia had slipped through his guard, and become as necessary to him as the air he breathed.

Ten

For the third time Marc glanced at the face of the grandfather clock in the foyer, and restlessly paced back to the foot of the staircase. He glanced toward the landing at a sound from above, and caught his breath as Tricia began to descend the stairs. Her flaxen hair was piled on top of her head in a mass of curls, held together with the diamond-studded comb he'd bought her for her birthday. Diamonds also sparkled against her small earlobes, and he recognized them as his last gift to her. Considering her refusal to accept the gems at the time, he was extraordinarily pleased to see her wearing them.

A simple white-gold chain circled her slender neck, and as she drew closer she seemed as delicate and lovely as a fairy princess girded with twinkling stars. He couldn't tear his eyes away from her—Tricia's face radiated a warmth that made him want to bask forever in her presence. He ran a finger beneath the collar of his ruffle-fronted white shirt, trying to ease the constriction caused by a hated bow tie. He had never been comfortable in formal dress, and he felt especially constrained in a tuxedo.

Tricia reached the bottom of the stairs, and glanced at him with obvious approval. "You look like a movie star," she teased.

"An ugly one," he retorted, but he gave her a sheepish grin as he held out his arm to her. "Shall we go, beauty?"

Pulling the silver-threaded stole she wore over her long gown more tightly around her, she assumed a regal air, and said, "Ready when you are, my elegant beast."

It didn't take them long to reach Peter Greer's estate, which was located in the hills quite close to their own property. As they drove through a pair of fussily ornate gates and negotiated the long circular drive fronting the Gothic-style house, Tricia remarked upon the view. "This place must make Mr. Greer feel like king of the mountain."

Helping her from the car, his mouth quirked cynically. "He acts like one most of the time."

Surprised by his disparaging tone, she glanced at him as they began climbing the stairs leading to a pair of double doors, which were undoubtedly the largest and most heavily carved she'd ever seen. Hesitantly she asked, "Don't you like him?"

Tricia clutched her evening bag tightly to her chest, praying he would admit to a dislike for their host. Right now she was nervous enough about meeting Alita Murray's esteemed uncle, and she would feel much better if she knew that Marc wouldn't be unduly influenced by the man's good opinion of him. She didn't want Marc doing business with that woman's relative, and with a twinge of shame she realized how prejudicial she was being. Unlike his niece, Mr. Greer would probably turn out to be perfectly charming.

That didn't prove to be the case, as Tricia discovered within minutes of meeting him. He was florid faced and heavy set, a short, stocky, loud-mouthed individual who made her cringe inwardly when he spoke. "You have a lovely wife, Everett. Just lovely."

At that moment, Alita rushed over to them as quickly as she could in a gold lamé gown tight enough to have been painted over her voluptuous curves. It certainly left nothing to the imagination, and when Marc turned to greet the other woman Tricia wanted to cover his eyes. She also wanted to cover his ears when the brazen witch murmured, "Darling, I thought you'd never arrive."

"As you can see," he returned mockingly, "my wife and I are both present and accounted for."

His gaze fell on Tricia's face as he spoke, and a warm tingle of pleasure swept through her at the tender grin he sent in her direction. Their gazes met and locked together for a moment, and the intimate message in his eyes was for her alone. She began to tremble, her increased heartbeat snatching at her breath.

But the poignant interlude was abruptly shattered by their host's booming voice. "It's a pleasure to meet you at last, Mrs. Everett."

Tricia's skin crawled as his protuberant eyes wandered over her with an impertinent stare, his fleshy mouth stretched in more of a leer than a smile. "I've heard a great deal about you from my niece. I was hoping we'd get acquainted when I visited the Bahamas, but I know not every woman trots along after her husband. I guess I was spoiled by my dearest Emily, who always put my welfare ahead of her own when she was alive."

What an obnoxious individual, Tricia decided angrily, and about as subtle as his sweet little niece. It seemed that Uncle Peter was firmly in Alita's corner, and he wouldn't be averse to helping her make Marc husband number two. With a good-mannered smile that threatened to crack her lips, she lied like the well-brought-up young woman she was. "I'm happy to meet you, Mr. Greer."

His pudgy fingers patted her arm, which fortunately was still covered by her shawl. Edging away from him, in desperation she turned her head toward Marc. But he was talking to another man who had just approached him, and all she managed to do was connect with a pair of hostile green eyes. The febrile glitter in their depths made her shiver with revulsion, unable to understand how such an outwardly beautiful woman could be so ugly inside.

Much to her relief, at that moment one of the maids approached Alita and began to wave her hands and speak in a voice shrill with agitation. With a grimace of annoyance Alita followed the other woman, presumably, judging from the little Tricia overheard, heading in the direction of the kitchen. Quickly, before her host had a chance to continue speaking to her, Tricia grasped Marc's hand in a silent plea for deliverance.

Instantly his arm came around her, and as he tucked her against his side another guest claimed Peter Greer's attention. Marc introduced her to the man he'd been talking to, and after a few minutes of desultory conversation a stern-visaged butler announced that dinner was served. As they headed toward the dining room, Marc paused before a smiling maid and reached for Tricia's shawl. Her back was to him as he slid it from her shoulders, and his shocked expulsion of breath wafted against her naked flesh.

Slowly he turned her around, his eyes widening in stupefaction as he glanced down at the plunging neckline. "What holds that thing up?" he questioned in amazement.

The maid giggled as she folded Tricia's shawl over her arm, quickly disappearing into an anteroom. Suddenly alone with her husband, she wished fervently that she'd never seen a certain cinnamon gown. "Willpower?" she replied faintly.

Marc's lips twitched, and he shook his head as though dazed. "Will you never cease to surprise me?"

"I'm sorry," she murmured guiltily. "I shouldn't have bought it. It's really not my style."

"Why?" he inquired softly. "You look exquisite."

Her eyes widened in amazement. "But you hate brown."

Bending closer, he murmured, "Then just think how much I'll enjoy taking it off of you."

After that, the night held a special radiance for Tricia. Marc hardly let her out of his sight, and as the hours passed she thought the electricity sparking between them must be evident to everyone around them. It was certainly evident to Alita, who became the only sour note in an otherwise delightful evening. Tricia couldn't escape her menacing glances or sarcastic smiles, but with Marc by her side she didn't let the other woman's antipathy bother her.

At least she didn't, until Alita cornered her in a powder room and proceeded to vent her spleen. "You think you're so clever," she hissed, "but you're fooling yourself. The only reason Marc is paying such marked attention to you is to throw you off the scent."

Tired of being baited by the other woman, she snapped, "You're talking nonsense, Alita."

"Am I?" she asked with a sneer. "Marc and I are lovers, and as soon as he can unload you we'll be married."

Blood rushed to Tricia's head and then receded with alarming suddenness, leaving her deathly pale. "You're lying."

"Marc and I have been having an affair for nearly a year," she stated bluntly. "With all the time he's spent away from home recently, surely your suspicions have been aroused."

Tricia's eyes narrowed. "You haven't known him that long."

"We were involved long before I started working for him."

She smiled, and tapped a blood-red fingernail against her teeth. "Let me see, part of July we spent together in France at the most charming little inn. You do remember the two weeks Marc was away from home last summer?"

Not waiting for Tricia to reply, she uttered a triumphant laugh and smoothed a languid hand over her hip. "And there was that chalet we shared in Colorado. We were there for nearly the entire month of December, if I remember correctly."

Her eyes stricken, Tricia remembered Marc being away from home in July, and in December he'd barely gotten back in time for Christmas. Was Alita telling the truth? she wondered, sickness clawing at her stomach. How else would she be privy to his movements, when she hadn't even worked for his firm until recently? Did he love this woman, and want to marry her as soon as he could conveniently rid himself of his present wife?

"It isn't true," she whispered. "Marc hasn't asked me for a divorce."

"But he will, because that's the price I'm going to demand for giving him what he needs."

Clenching her hands into fists at her sides, Tricia asked, "What are you talking about?"

A smug smile curved Alita's mouth, and her eyes glittered with an almost feral light. "I'm talking about the help Marc needs from my uncle, if he wishes to keep out of the bankruptcy courts."

Straightening defensively, Tricia refused to falter. "A man planning a project the size of the Bahamian resort is hardly destitute," she retorted. "You're making all of this up in an attempt to cause trouble between Marc and me."

"Don't you have any pride?" Alita accused with a disdainful toss of her head. "If I were in your shoes I would be the one demanding a divorce. I'd be damned before I would hang around and let any man dump me for another woman."

Angling her chin pugnaciously, Tricia remarked with quiet certainty, "That's not going to happen."

"It will if I have anything to say about it, and believe me, I do. Why do you think the Bahamian resort project is so vitally important to Marc?"

Tricia was stunned into silence, and Alita used the opportunity to further her claims with the cruel ruthlessness of a woman with little to lose and a great deal to gain. She said that Marc had been overextending himself for years, and that several of his most recent endeavors had sent him further into debt.

"He made the mistake of only paying penalties and interest payments to the IRS," she continued in clipped accents, "and now they're demanding payment in full. Nearly all of his funds are tied up, and to try to liquidate his assets now would complete his financial ruin.

"So far the news media hasn't gotten wind of his embarrassing difficulties, and with my uncle's financial backing they never will. Peter's money will assure the completion of the resort, and Marc will be able to ride out his current cash flow problems with ease.

"If you really love him you won't try to stand in his way," Alita concluded on a note of triumph. "He'd only end up hating you, and you'll lose him to me either way."

With a final toss of her head, the other woman turned and left Tricia at the mercy of her thoughts.

The seeds of doubt had been planted in Tricia's mind, and a final episode had placed the seal on her despondency. Desperate to discover the extent of Alita's hold over her husband, on the way home she asked him to replace her with another contract lawyer. He immediately stiffened, his voice a harshly accusing rasp. "Alita was afraid of something like this, but it's not going to happen, Patricia. Your jealousy has no place in my business decisions, and Alita is an excellent employee. I have no reason to fire her."

BIG SUMMER READ

Summer Reading At Its Best

In July, Harlequin and Silhouette bring readers the Big Summer Read Program. Heat up your summer with these four exciting new novels by top Harlequin and Silhouette authors.

SOMEWHERE IN TIME by Barbara Bretton
YESTERDAY COMES TOMORROW by Rebecca Flanders
A DAY IN APRIL by Mary Lynn Baxter
LOVE CHILD by Patricia Coughlin

From time travel to fame and fortune, this program offers something for everyone.

Available at your favorite retail outlet.

FREE GIFT OFFER

With Free Gift Promotion proofs-of-purchase from Harlequin or Silhouette, you can receive this beautiful jewelry collection. Each item is perfect by itself, or collect all three for a complete jewelry ensemble.

For a classic look that is always in style, this beautiful gold tone jewelry will complement any outfit. Items include:

Gold tone clip earrings (approx. retail value $9.95), a 7½" gold tone bracelet (approx. retail value $15.95) and a 18" gold tone necklace (approx. retail value $29.95).

FREE GIFT OFFER TERMS

To receive your free gift, complete the certificate according to directions. Be certain to enclose the required number of Free Gift proofs-of-purchase, which are found on the last page of every specially marked Free Gift Harlequin or Silhouette romance novel. Requests must be received no later than July 31, 1992. Items depicted are for illustrative purposes only and may not be exactly as shown. Please allow 6 to 8 weeks for receipt of order. Offer good while quantities of gifts last. In the event an ordered gift is no longer available, you will receive a free, previously unpublished Harlequin or Silhouette book for every proof-of-purchase you have submitted with your request, plus a refund of the postage-and-handling charge you have included. Offer good in the U.S. and Canada only.

MILLIONAIRE *Sweepstakes* !

As an added value every time you send in a completed certificate with the correct number of proofs-of-purchase, your name will automatically be entered in our Million Dollar Sweepstakes. The more completed offer certificates you send in, the more often your name will be entered in our sweepstakes and the better your chances of winning.

PRO1

"She . . . she's your mistress, isn't she?"

"I'm not even going to bother answering that question," he stated curtly.

Shaking her head, she remarked dully, "Then it's true."

With a snarl of rage, he muttered, "Believe what the hell you want."

Swallowing past the lump in her throat, she whispered, "Don't I matter to you at all? The woman's been rude to me from the moment we met, and yet it's me you're angry with."

"According to Alita, you took an instant aversion to her."

Tricia stared down at her hands, which were clenched into fists in her lap. "And you choose to take her word over mine?"

"I don't fancy a ring through my nose, Patricia."

"How about the one on your left hand?" she cried bitterly. "Do you fancy that?"

They were stopped at a signal light, and he turned a grim, harshly unforgiving face in her direction. "I'm beginning to wonder if this emotional seesaw you've got me on is worth the effort," he remarked heavily. "I'm really beginning to wonder."

A single tear fell on the back of her hand, and soon another followed. Eventually they were running down her ashen cheeks in a torrent, and Marc uttered a disgusted curse when he glanced in her direction. "First you use sex and now tears to get your own way," he accused her furiously. "What did you think, that you'd turn me into a tame puppy willing to roll over at the snap of your fingers, my dear? As you can see, that's not the case."

"No," she responded faintly. "It's not, is it?"

"Dammit . . . what do you want from me?"

"It doesn't matter," she muttered. "I don't want to talk about it anymore."

A week later Marc left for the Bahamas, and since Cully's new grandbaby decided to arrive on the day he was to depart, Tricia drove him to the airport. The porter checked his luggage at the curbside, and after Marc uttered a curt goodbye he disappeared inside the terminal building. As she watched him through the wall of glass, a striking, dark-haired woman joined him near the airline ticket counter. Tricia didn't stay to see them walk toward the departure gate together. The dull apathy that had become so familiar to Tricia suddenly shattered, and as she returned to her car her only need was to escape from the pain.

Eleven

For once the rugged beauty of more than fifty miles of California's Pacific coastline failed to ease Tricia's troubled mind, and she drove toward the cabin Marc had bought for her as a wedding present with her thoughts in turmoil. Signs passed by her in a blur, indicating other picturesque towns south of Montara Mountain. They were places she'd visited with her parents as a child, and as familiar to her as her own reflection.

This area was where she'd chosen to spend her honeymoon. Although Marc had been appalled by her preference, he had cancelled the reservations he'd made for Cancún and arranged for them to stay at a small bed and breakfast inn near Moss Beach. Of course in those early days of their marriage, she recalled bitterly, Marc had been intent on pleasing her.

But since he'd chosen to take Alita's word over hers, that obviously wasn't the case any longer. With an inevitability she should have been able to predict by now, such a thought placed a lump in her throat and brought tears to her eyes. Gripping the steering wheel until her knuckles turned white, she silently remonstrated with herself as she blinked back the threatening moisture.

Over the past several hours she'd shed enough tears to float a barge, and in time, she stopped indulging in useless bouts of self-pity. Feeling sorry for herself wasn't going to heal the wounds Marc had inflicted on her heart and her pride. Nor would it help her decide what she was going to do with the rest of her life if he chose to divorce her and marry Alita.

Just the possibility of having to endure a future without the man she loved caused a dry sob to tear from her throat, which was already raw and sore from weeping. She had to regain control over her emotions, she told herself sternly. She needed to wipe the confusion from her thoughts if she wished to function with any clarity of mind, which was why she'd sought out the one place in the world she considered a haven.

Feeling suddenly claustrophobic, she uttered a pithy curse she'd never imagined herself using before today, and reached for the button that would roll down her driver's side window. She inhaled deeply, the brine-scented air filling her lungs and instilling a measure of calm to her jagged nerves. All around her were flowers encompassing the colors of a rainbow, and the visual feast both delighted and saddened her.

Tricia automatically lessened her speed as she approached the outskirts of Pescadero, suddenly eager to stock up on provisions and reach her cabin. She and Marc had visited the straw flower fields while on their honeymoon. They had been inspecting a huge, galvanized metal shed used to dry and sort the blooms, when they learned about a nearby property for sale. Though she'd recognized a sales pitch when she heard one, she hadn't been able to help herself from turning a hopeful gaze in Marc's direction.

With an indulgent smile, he asked, "Want to take a look?"

She caught her breath. "Could we?" she whispered excitedly.

When he nodded, her eyes widened, and she'd nearly bubbled over with joy. As they walked back to their car she had been chattering freely, forgetting the shy awkwardness she'd thus far displayed in his presence. "Don't get your hopes up, Patricia," he eventually warned. "Quite a few of the places in this area are in bad shape, and not worth the outrageous prices their owners expect to receive."

But derelict or not, she had fallen in love with the small, three-roomed log cabin on sight. Far back from the scarred and pitted excuse that passed for a county road, the small structure was set in a clearing and was dwarfed by the forest that surrounded it on three sides. The structure seemed sound enough from a distance, even though it leaned a little drunkenly to one side and possessed some very odd if endearingly quaint angles.

"Whoever built this place was certainly no architect," Marc muttered derisively.

No sooner were the words out of his mouth than a shaft of sunlight broke free of the fog bank that had formed a cloud cover over the sky all morning. Its rays bounced off the cabin's grime-smudged windows, and she laughed out loud as their car bumped and rattled over the steep, uneven driveway. "Look, it's winking at us, Marc."

He pulled up in front and slanted a wry glance in her direction, not even bothering to shut off the engine. But his features grew soft as he studied her flushed cheeks and sparkling, bluebonnet eyes. "Do you like it?" he questioned doubtfully, without attempting to exit the car.

She looked from him to the little house that seemed to be welcoming them, and uttered a heartfelt sigh as she nodded an affirmative. Without another word he turned the car around and headed back down the drive, leaving her staring at him in surprise. Disappointed that he hadn't been interested enough to get out and look around, she asked dispiritedly, "Where are we going?"

He had pointed toward a dilapidated sign, half standing, half lying in a patch of weeds, and said, "Into town to look up the real estate agent."

Tricia sighed at the memory as she began to drive through Pescadero's main thoroughfare, relieved by the diversion which the quaint town, with its white buildings and quietly rustic streets, provided. She felt like a traveler returning home after a long absence, and a feeling of belonging cheered her flagging spirits as nothing else could have.

Tricia pulled up in front of a sturdy, slightly lopsided building and cut her engine. Pocketing the keys, she stepped from the car and glanced around her. The store was run by an elderly couple who had befriended her when she'd first started coming up here, both of them fourth generation Pescaderians. Although she definitely paid more for her purchases, she much preferred the informal atmosphere of the little store to that of an impersonal supermarket.

"Why, Mrs. Everett," a trilling voice cried out when a tinkling bell above the door heralded her arrival. "We haven't seen you in a month of Sundays."

Approaching the long, weathered counter, which was burdened with an assortment of candy jars and dried beans, as well as a huge, ugly metallic green cash register that had seen better days, she returned the other woman's smile. "Hello, Mrs. Alves," she said. "I'm glad to be back."

The spry, gray-haired proprietress bustled about and began helping Tricia select what she would need for a week's stay, chattering irrepressively as she did so. Tricia soon caught up on all the local gossip, and when Mr. Alves entered from the back room to box up her purchases, he added a few tidbits of his own.

He finally concluded with, "Mama and I are going poke-poling after church on Sunday. She's fixing a picnic lunch for us and the kids and grandkids, and there's more than enough for one more. Why don't you come along and see how it's done?"

She'd once heard the term "poke-poling", and had asked Mr. Alves to satisfy her curiosity. Discovering that the idea was to catch monkey-face eels in the tide pools located at the south end of Pescadero State Beach, a great deal of her enthusiasm had waned. But she'd politely hidden her revulsion from the friendly shopkeeper, and now she was paying for her duplicity. "I don't think—" she began weakly.

"That you should intrude on a family outing," Mrs. Alves interrupted with a derisive sniff, her wide grin showing a charmingly crooked front tooth. "But that's nonsense, isn't it, Papa? We'd love to have you."

By the time her groceries were loaded into the car, Tricia had arranged to meet the Alves family in front of the Pescadero Community Church. Built of wood in 1867 and expressing the Greek Revival architectural style, the building was a California historical landmark and easy to find. "What can I bring, Mrs. Alves?" she asked with a shade more enthusiasm.

"Warm clothing, a waterproof jacket, and your pretty self," she was told, in stern tones belied by a pair of twinkling black eyes. "And call me Alicia," she insisted just as firmly. "Papa's name is Manuel."

"My name's Tricia," she replied with a grin.

Although she had been hesitant about accepting the Alves's invitation, when she drove away from the store she felt her spirits uplifted by a sense of belonging. She hummed beneath her breath as she cleaned the cabin and arranged her groceries in the few cupboards the tiny kitchen could boast, the rest relegated to the screened-in back porch where shelves had been placed for temporary storage.

When she finally finished, it was getting dark. She was too tired to do more than eat a hastily contrived meal, and then she headed for the bathroom to shower. After cleaning her teeth and running a brush through her hair, she glanced around the plain room as she smoothed moisturizer into her skin. As her hands absently worked the cream into her cheeks, she couldn't help comparing the bathroom's Spartan simplicity with the lushness of the one at home.

When the real estate agent had shown them around, Marc had wanted to practically gut everything and start from scratch. Horrified at the prospect, she'd quickly talked him out of making any immediate improvements. "I think it's charming just the way it is," she informed him anxiously.

Although he hadn't seemed upset by her preference in decor, she wondered now if a lack of creature comforts had given him an aversion to the place. It was possible, she supposed, wandering into the bedroom with a thoughtful frown crinkling her forehead. She spent every weekend she could spare here regardless of the weather, but Marc had never once accompanied her. Every time she'd asked, he had used the pressure of work as an excuse to decline, and she'd finally started planning her visits to coincide with the times he was away from home on business.

But more than likely he'd been avoiding spending any time alone with her, she decided apathetically, pulling a sturdy pair of flannel pajamas from a tall dresser positioned in the far corner of the long room. She sniffed as the thought brought tears to her eyes, and instantly became distracted by the pungent aroma that rose to her nostrils.

She was oddly comforted by the familiar scent of cedar that permeated the entire cabin, especially during warm weather. It was no wonder, since nearly all of the furniture she'd chosen had been fashioned from the fragrant wood at her request. It was an odor she associated with coziness, serenity, and peace of mind, and she deliberately pushed aside thoughts of Marc as she finished dressing.

Her long-sleeved, long-legged pajamas were toasty warm, as was the four-poster after her body heat took the chill from the sheets. As she relaxed upon a fluffy feather pillow, she pulled the covers all the way up to her chin and yawned. She kept the antiquated wall heater in the hall turned off at night. Being familiar with the area, she knew that by morning the dense fog rolling in from the ocean would have considerably lowered the temperature both indoors and out. Burrowing even deeper under the heavy blankets, she rolled over onto her side and closed her eyes. Sleep claimed her before she had a chance to worry about anything else.

By the time Sunday rolled around Tricia was in a much calmer frame of mind, largely due to her decision to return home and fight like hell to save her marriage. After hours spent watching the rhythmic pulse of waves pounding into shore on the beach, and tramping through the woods behind the cabin, she had reached the conclusion that she was through being an emotional coward. She was damned if Alita Murray was going to snatch her husband away from her, not if she had anything to say about it! Because no matter how confident the other woman had sounded, in her heart Tricia knew that no one could be a better wife to Marc than she was.

The certainty buoyed up her flagging spirits as nothing else could have, and she thoroughly enjoyed her day with the Alves family. That gregarious clan was comprised of two stocky sons, their wives, one as yet unmarried daughter and her fiancé, and sundry children in assorted shapes and sizes. She cuddled Marita and Paul's baby, and ached for her own as she stared down at his sweet face. She absorbed the closeness and camaraderie of the happy family, and wondered why she and Marc couldn't find the contentment in each other that Alicia and Manuel had discovered.

But she wasn't given the time to brood about her thoughts. The twins, James and John, took her on an oceanographic excursion along the beach, where they elicited her help in trying to find a globose dune beetle for a science project at school. Since this necessitated scrambling over active sand dunes, where leaf litter of coastal scrub vegetation provided a habitat for the rare beetles, her back and legs were aching by the time the energetic teens agreed to return to the picnic site for dinner.

She and the boys never found their elusive prey, but at least it had gotten her out of poke-poling. As they rejoined the others, who had appropriated a couple of large picnic tables for their use, she found herself surveying the homey scene with thought-provoking intensity. It was difficult to believe that the Portola Expedition had camped on this very beach so long ago, and that this sandy and rocky shoreline had once been a favored launching site for whaling boats.

Everyone lent a hand in setting the food out on the tables, and after what could only be described as a sumptuous feast they then rested and enjoyed the end of a perfect day. The smaller children, worn out from their exhausting play, slept nearby on homemade quilts, while the hardier souls talked lazily as they waited for the sun to disappear over the horizon.

Breathtaking streaks of vermillion and purple tangled together against a rapidly darkening backdrop of blue, the amazing kaleidoscope reflecting off puffy white clouds. Deep rose and pink streaks still bathed the evening sky as they repacked the Alves's minivan for the return trip into town, a fantasy array that lingered in Tricia's mind long after she had arrived back at the cabin.

The porch light had burned out, but she'd left the lamp in the living room on in anticipation of her return. The muted glow through the lacy curtains covering the wide front window was a welcome sight as she parked the car, and there was a tired but contented smile on her face as she climbed the few steps leading up to the wooden railed porch.

She was just fitting her key into the lock when the door was pulled open from inside, and she almost died of fright when a furious voice burst out, "Where in the hell have you been, woman?"

Tricia dropped the cardigan that was draped over her arm and clutched at her chest. Staring at the lean, rigidly angry face in front of her, she questioned stupidly, "Where's your car?"

"Out back," he replied with gritty voiced terseness as he studied her disheveled appearance with disparaging thoroughness. With stiffly uncoordinated movements, he picked up her sweater, and gestured her inside. "Where have you been, Tricia?" he asked again. "You've had me half out of my mind with worry."

Her legs shook as she responded to his unspoken command, and at the click of the door she whirled around to face him. The sight of her limp, bedraggled sweater clutched in his fist struck her funny, and all of a sudden she was howling uncontrollably. The laughter rose to a piercing level, her eyes watering as she struggled to catch her breath.

Suddenly the sweater sailed through the air to land on the back of a kitchen chair, and Marc was shaking her until she thought her neck would snap. Now the tears spurting from her eyes were real, born of hysteria and grief and a crazy kind of inner relief. But the happiness she'd felt at her first sight of him soon gave way to a satisfying burst of temper, and she began to pound on his chest with all the strength left to her. "I hate you," she cried, her voice breaking on a sob.

If possible, his features became even more grim as she threw those words at him, but all he said was, "No you don't."

"Will you... let me go?" she demanded through gritted teeth. "I can't... breathe."

Although he stopped shaking her silly, he refused to release her. Her shoulders ached from the fierce grip of his hands, and her anger rose to new heights. "Don't tell me how I feel, you... you traitor!"

"What the hell are you talking about?"

Her chin rose mutinously as her eyes flashed fire. "I'm talking about the... arrangement you have with Alita Murray."

At this he went absolutely still, his darkly brooding gaze intent on her face as he asked softly, "What arrangement, Tricia?"

Twelve

Tricia shook her head with sluggish tiredness, and ran trembling fingers through her tousled hair. Averting her head to the side, she stared down at the naked fireplace cavity and sighed dispiritedly. "Could we talk later?" she asked. "I've spent the day on the beach, and I'd like to bathe and change into clothing a little less gritty than these."

Something in her voice must have told him she was on the point of collapse, because his hold gentled as he guided her toward the bathroom. "Go soak in the tub while I get you a nightgown."

Resentful even in the face of his surprising gentleness, she snapped, "I wear pajamas when I'm here."

"Then where do you keep them?"

He sounded so calm and sensible he made her feel like a shrew, and she tried to sound a touch more reasonable when she answered his question. Unfortunately she only managed to appear petulant as she muttered grudgingly, "Under my pillow."

In an exhausted daze she filled the tub and stripped off her jeans and yellow, long-sleeved shirt, grimacing as sand spilled from them to the floor. Since the damage was already done, she grabbed a brush from the top drawer of the basin cabinet and bent over to vigorously brush her hair. With her head upside down she didn't hear Marc's return, a muffled expletive her first indication of his presence.

With a gasp she straightened, her hair a wild, white gold cloud around her pinkening cheeks as her brain started functioning again on all cylinders. Grabbing the nearest available covering, which just happened to be a small hand towel, she spread it in front of herself and glared at him. "If you don't mind, I'd appreciate a little privacy."

"But I do mind."

Crossing his arms over his chest he leaned his hip against the basin, his gaze wandering over her at will. "The way I see it, you're in quite a predicament, sweetheart. You can either cover your lovely breasts, or that sweet tangle of golden curls, but not both. I'm dying to see how you choose to solve the problem."

With an exasperated growl she turned, and quickly rearranged the towel to cover her backside. His voice quivering with amusement, he whispered, "Now how are you going to turn off the faucets without bending over?''

Stamping her foot, she sent him a pleading glance over her shoulder. "Will you get out of here?''

Something in the way she looked at him managed to resurrect his animosity, because his mouth tightened into a scowl of displeasure. Dropping her pajamas on top of a wicker laundry hamper, he spun on his heel and left without another word. Tamping down a momentary twinge of regret, Tricia turned off the water and stepped into the overly full tub.

She laid back slowly, afraid the water would tip over the edge. Once she was satisfied that the floor was safe, she sighed and let heat permeate every bone in her tired and aching body. Yet she couldn't seem to ease the tension that had risen inside of her at her first sight of Marc, and nor could she stop the endless questions from revolving in her mind.

But like the coward she was, the last thing she wanted to do was talk to him. Explanations meant confessions, and she didn't think she could bear to hear him admit to an affair with that she-wolf, Alita. She had planned on what she would say to him when she returned home, but his sudden appearance had caused every scenario she'd thought up to seep right out of her brain.

What would she do if he really did want a divorce? As the thought crept into her mind, she sat up with an abruptness that finally sent a wave of water onto the floor. She was muttering beneath her breath when

Marc reappeared in the doorway, his forehead wrinkled into a concerned frown. "What was that hideous noise?" he asked. "Did you fall?"

"No, I did not fall," she retorted sarcastically. "If you really want to know, I slammed my fist against the wall."

"In a temper, are you?"

Shielding her breasts with her arms, she glared at his grinning face. "Damned right I am, and if you don't disappear again you're going to be sorry."

The childishness of the taunt made her cringe, but no more than the warning glint in his dark eyes as he slowly approached her. "Just what are you planning to do, bean me with a loofah?"

"I'm planning to divorce you!"

Where the words came from Tricia had no idea. As she saw Marc's expression change, she wished she had bitten off her tongue before uttering that damning remark. "Like hell," he murmured softly, his hands going to his belt. "Like hell you will!"

Moistening her lips with the tip of her tongue, she asked, "What are you doing?"

"I need a shower."

Instantly Tricia jumped to her feet, and tried to wrap herself in the plastic shower curtain that hung from a rail over the tub. "Then I'll just leave and let you...."

The rest of his clothes were systematically dispensed with, and joined hers on the floor. She stared at his body in shock, but there was also undeniable hunger in the eyes that roamed compulsively over his naked frame. With a start of surprise she felt her fingers being pried loose from the shower curtain, and then he was inside the tub with her and the plastic was closing out the rest of the world.

With his big toe he pried loose the plug stuck in the drain, and as the tub began to empty he reached for the faucets. Soon they were enveloped in a torrent of water, and his big body had her backed against the cool tile of the wall. "Now," he murmured gently, bracing his hands on either side of her head. "Why don't you tell me what arrangement I have with Alita Murray?"

Biting her lip, she lowered her eyes to his hair-roughened chest. "I know you've overextended yourself, Marc. You don't have to hide the truth from me any longer."

"Mmm," he murmured, pressing his mouth against her forehead. "So I'm broke, am I?"

"N-not exactly, but Alita told me you could lose everything if this Bahamian project fails."

In the process of nibbling her ear, he straightened with unexpected swiftness and met her troubled gaze. "Is this where the arrangement with Alita comes in?"

"W-with her uncle, really."

She tried to avert her face, needing to escape from his piercingly intent inspection. But before she could do so, his large hand was gripping her chin. When he tilted her head back, water rushed up her nose and she began to choke. "Oh, my Lord," he exclaimed with a laugh. "I intended to lighten the mood by sharing your shower, not drown you."

"You couldn't prove it by me," she muttered between coughs.

He grabbed a bar of soap from a nearby dish and thrust it at her.

"Finish what you have to do before you strangle to death, but don't imagine you're getting out of this conversation, Patricia. I'll meet you in the living room in exactly ten minutes. We can talk then. And if you're not there I'll come back and personally drown you!"

Tricia made it in time, but only because she'd forgone the blow dryer, deciding to towel dry her hair instead. Entering the living room with assumed nonchalance, she curled up against one corner of the couch. Marc was standing at the window looking out, his posture as rigid as the arm that was braced against the window frame. His hair had been towel-dried and combed into its usual order, but he hadn't taken the time to dress.

Instead he was wearing a short, silky black robe, and his legs and feet were as bare as her own. She swallowed heavily, realizing that he was most likely as naked as a jaybird underneath the skimpy covering. With an abruptness that startled her he turned, and she caught her breath at the expression on his face.

Marc appeared tired and dispirited, but that wasn't what caught her attention so forcefully. It was the shadow of pain she could see in his eyes, and the vulnerability expressed in the downward curve of his lips that caused her heart to begin beating wildly on an upsurge of hope. He looked as miserable as she felt, and suddenly she was desperate to hear what he had to say.

Her voice trembled as she whispered, "I'm ready, Marc."

"Are you?" He walked toward her with slowly measured footsteps, his eyes never leaving her face. "I wonder if I am."

She studied the exhausted lethargy of his movements as he sat beside her, concern deepening the blue of her eyes as she became fully aware of the extent of his depression. "What do you mean?" she questioned softly. "I thought you came here to get everything out into the open."

Leaning forward he braced his elbows on his splayed knees, and clasped his hands between them. He was staring down at them when he asked, "By everything, I suppose you're referring to my affair with Alita Murray?"

Tricia drew a breath inward, the sound loud enough to emphasize her dismay. "She told me you want a divorce. Is that true?"

In barely audible tones, he asked, "Isn't that what you want?"

When he angled his head to glance at her, she carefully controlled her features. "No," she murmured as she quickly shifted her attention to the floor. "No, it's not what I want, Marc."

"Even though Alita told you we've been having an affair?"

"Even though," she admitted in choked accents. "If...if you want to end things with her and stay with me, I...promise to do my best to make our marriage work."

"You'd forgive me?"

"For cheating on me?" Her mouth twisted with momentary bitterness, but the words she uttered were as forgiving as he could have wished. "It wasn't entirely your fault that you turned to another woman," she sighed despondently. "I've never been much of a wife to you."

"Look at me, Tricia," he demanded suddenly.

She did as he asked, and she nearly cried out in shock. There was a sheen of moisture glistening in his dark eyes, and anguish in his voice as he said, "You have been more of a wife than I ever deserved, my darling. You are the only wife I want, and the only wife I'll ever want."

A sob tore free from her throat, and suddenly she was in his arms. Her face pressed against his chest, she cried, "I love you, Marc. I love you so much, and I didn't know how I was going to bear living without you."

Cradling her head against the crook of his arm, he feathered his lips against her forehead. His eyes were closed, the eyelashes dampened from his own tears, and she stared up at him in wonder. "You...you're crying," she gasped.

"I almost lost you, and all because I was afraid to tell you how much you mean to me. If I had, Alita would never have been able to get to you with her lies."

She reached out and grabbed at his arm, her entire body stiffening. "Lies?"

His lashes rose, and a compassionate smile eased the severity of his expression. "There was no affair, my love. Hell, there wasn't even a one-night stand, not that she didn't try while we were in the Bahamas. But I could never do to you what my mother did to my father, Tricia."

It was said so simply, without embellishment, and yet she believed him unconditionally. Why hadn't she realized the truth for herself? she wondered guiltily, especially after she had learned how disgusted Marc had been by his mother's affairs. Dear God, how much pain she could have saved herself...saved them both!

Turning her head slightly, she placed a kiss against his chest. "I'm sorry for believing Alita's lies, but they sounded so plausible, Marc. I was even fooled into believing that the two of you were involved long before she went to work for you. She came up with times you'd been away from home, and even mentioned the places where you'd stayed."

"Not difficult to do, when you're privy to a firm's expense accounts and past tax records."

Wryly she admitted, "I should have thought of that."

Cupping her cheek in his warm palm, he brushed the tears from her skin with the pad of his thumb. "What else did she tell you? We might as well flush all the monsters from under the bed while we're about it."

Shamefaced, she replied to his question. "She told me you were on shaky ground financially, and that without her uncle's help you'd go under."

He uttered a snort and shook his head. "Alita's an accomplished liar, I'll say that for her. But none of what she told you has any basis in truth, love. The Bahamian project is going ahead as scheduled, and I never needed her uncle's help to realize my goals. I had him investigated, and when I read the reports last week I decided against accepting him as an investor. And by the way, my corporation is more than solvent enough to pick up the slack, Tricia. A smart businessman never bets everything on a single toss of the dice. If the Bahamian project were to fail, it wouldn't beggar me—not by a long shot."

"But I had no way of knowing that," she cried. "You've always refused to discuss your work with me, Mark."

Instantly his features hardened, his mouth assuming a grim cast.

"Yes, and by doing so, I left you open for Alita's treachery. I blame myself for the pain she caused you, but I'll try and make it up to you. For starters, I'll be hiring a new corporate lawyer to replace Alita, and if she ever comes near you again, she'll wish she'd never been born."

Tricia's eyes closed briefly as she sighed in relief, and when they opened again, they were once more filled with moisture.

"Oh, Mark," she replied brokenly. "I'm so sorry for allowing Alita to make me a victim, but everything she said seemed to reinforce her position. She told me that her price for convincing her uncle to help you was marriage, and she said you'd end up hating me if I stood in your way."

"So you were supposed to leave me and file for a divorce, hmm?"

When she nodded, he looked murderous. "She overplayed her hand with that one. Obviously she never imagined I'd care enough to come after you."

"But you did," she whispered softly. "I should have confronted you with her lies, but I was too afraid of being told to my face that you didn't want me anymore."

"Of course you believed the conniving little witch," he muttered harshly. "Why wouldn't you? She covered all of the bases, and I played right into her hands by not denying that she and I were lovers when you asked."

She frowned in confusion, her expression puzzled as she met his eyes. "Why didn't you deny it, Marc?"

He lifted her into a sitting position, but his hands were tender on her shoulders as he held her away from him. "By then I knew just how much I loved you, and I was afraid you'd realize how weak I was where you were concerned."

"That's why you refused to fire Alita," she gasped. "You didn't want me to think that I could lead you around by the nose."

He smiled briefly at the comparison, but almost immediately his features grew somber. "The way my mother did my father," he admitted gruffly. "His love made him so damned vulnerable, and year after year I watched him deteriorate from a strong, good man with pride and dignity into a drunk who had to beg and plead for any crumbs of affection she was willing to give him. When she finally left him for her latest lover, my father couldn't take it."

Tensing, she whispered, "Marc, how did your father die?"

He stared past her shoulder at a horror only he could see. "He bought a gun and blew his brains out while I was at school. Cully heard the shot and called the police, but I arrived home before the authorities got there. The old man wrestled me to the ground to prevent me from seeing my father."

Inhaling sharply, he said, "I'll always be grateful to him for that, and to both him and Martha for providing me with a home until I turned eighteen."

"Oh, dear God!"

Her anguished exclamation drew him from the ugly specters of his past, and in an excess of need he reached out and pulled her against his trembling body. "All my life I swore that no woman would ever have that kind of power over me. Then I met you, and I wanted you desperately."

Rubbing his cheek against the softness of her hair, he confessed, "That's why my proposal was in the nature of a soulless bargain, because I couldn't admit, even to myself, how much you meant to me."

"Don't despise your father, Marc."

Her quietly spoken request surprised him, and he pulled back slightly so he could search her face. With a tenderness that was reflected in her eyes, she whispered, "It was his indulgence in alcohol that made him weak, not his feelings for your mother. Depression caused by a deadly disease made him end his own life, not her desertion. Otherwise he would never have placed such a terrible burden on the son who loved him."

With a muttered exclamation his head bent, and he buried his face in the hollow of her throat. "I can forgive him now," he said brokenly. "As long as I have you, I can forgive the whole damn world."

Instantly she grabbed him by the hair and shoved his head back, her scowl belied by a pair of twinkling eyes. "But not Alita Murray?"

Lifting her in his arms, he began to carry her toward the bedroom. "Never," he promised fervently. "Never in a million years, my dear."

For once, Tricia wasn't in the least annoyed or intimidated by that particular endearment. With her mouth against his warm brown throat, she confronted a truth she would never again doubt. She was his dear, she thought contentedly, just as he was hers.

* * * * *

The spirit of motherhood is the spirit of love—and how better to capture that special feeling than in our short story collection...

to
Mother
with
Love
'92

Curtiss Ann Matlock
Carole Halston
Linda Shaw

Three glorious new stories that embody the very essence of family and romance are contained in this heartfelt tribute to Mother. Share in the joy by joining us and three of your favorite Silhouette authors for this celebration of motherhood and romance.

Available at your favorite retail outlet in May.

SMD92

Take 4 bestselling love stories FREE
Plus get a FREE surprise gift!

Special Limited-time Offer

Mail to Silhouette Reader Service™

In the U.S.
3010 Walden Avenue
P.O. Box 1867
Buffalo, N.Y. 14269-1867

In Canada
P.O. Box 609
Fort Erie, Ontario
L2A 5X3

YES! Please send me 4 free Silhouette Desire® novels and my free surprise gift. Then send me 6 brand-new novels every month, which I will receive months before they appear in bookstores. Bill me at the low price of $2.49* each—a savings of 40¢ apiece off the cover prices. There are no shipping, handling or other hidden costs. I understand that accepting the books and gift places me under no obligation ever to buy any books. I can always return a shipment and cancel at any time. Even if I never buy another book from Silhouette, the 4 free books and the surprise gift are mine to keep forever.

*Offer slightly different in Canada—$2.49 per book plus 69¢ per shipment for delivery. Canadian residents add applicable federal and provincial sales tax. Sales tax applicable in N.Y.

225 BPA ADMA

326 BPA ADMP

Name _____ (PLEASE PRINT)

Address _____ Apt. No. _____

City _____ State/Prov. _____ Zip/Postal Code. _____

This offer is limited to one order per household and not valid to present Silhouette Desire® subscribers. Terms and prices are subject to change.

DES-92

© 1990 Harlequin Enterprises Limited

FREE GIFT OFFER

To receive your free gift, send us the specified number of proofs-of-purchase from any specially marked Free Gift Offer Harlequin or Silhouette book with the Free Gift Certificate properly completed, plus a check or money order (do not send cash) to cover postage and handling payable to Harlequin/Silhouette Free Gift Promotion Offer. We will send you the specified gift.

FREE GIFT CERTIFICATE

ITEM	A. GOLD TONE EARRINGS	B. GOLD TONE BRACELET	C. GOLD TONE NECKLACE
# of proofs-of-purchase required	3	6	9
Postage and Handling	$1.75	$2.25	$2.75
Check one	☐	☐	☐

Name: _____

Address: _____

City: _____ State: _____ Zip Code: _____

Mail this certificate, specified number of proofs-of-purchase and a check or money order for postage and handling to: HARLEQUIN/SILHOUETTE FREE GIFT OFFER 1992, P.O. Box 9057, Buffalo, NY 14269-9057. Requests must be received by July 31, 1992.

PLUS—Every time you submit a completed certificate with the correct number of proofs-of-purchase, you are automatically entered in our MILLION DOLLAR SWEEPSTAKES! No purchase or obligation necessary to enter. See below for alternate means of entry and how to obtain complete sweepstakes rules.

MILLION DOLLAR SWEEPSTAKES
NO PURCHASE OR OBLIGATION NECESSARY TO ENTER

To enter, hand-print (mechanical reproductions are not acceptable) your name and address on a 3″×5″ card and mail to Million Dollar Sweepstakes 6097, c/o either P.O. Box 9056, Buffalo, NY 14269-9056 or P.O. Box 621, Fort Erie, Ontario L2A 5X3. Limit: one entry per envelope. Entries must be sent via 1st-class mail. For eligibility, entries must be received no later than March 31, 1994. No liability is assumed for printing errors, lost, late or misdirected entries.

Sweepstakes is open to persons 18 years of age or older. All applicable laws and regulations apply. Sweepstakes offer void wherever prohibited by law. Prizewinners will be determined no later than May 1994. Chances of winning are determined by the number of entries distributed and received. For a copy of the Official Rules governing this sweepstakes offer, send a self-addressed, stamped envelope (WA residents need not affix return postage) to: Million Dollar Sweepstakes Rules, P.O. Box 4733, Blair, NE 68009.

SD1U

ONE PROOF-OF-PURCHASE
To collect your fabulous FREE GIFT you must include the necessary FREE GIFT proofs-of-purchase with a properly completed offer certificate.

(See center insert for details)